THE VOYAGE OF THE WHITE CLOUD

M. DARUSHA WEHM

The Voyage of the White Cloud
by M. Darusha Wehm

published by *in potentia* press 2018

ISBN 978-0-9951048-1-5

NOVELS

Beautiful Red
Children of Arkadia
The Voyage of the White Cloud

Andersson Dexter novels:
Self Made
Act of Will
The Beauty of Our Weapons
Pixels and Flesh

SHORT FICTION

Modern Love and other stories

MAINSTREAM FICTION BY DARUSHA WEHM

The Home for Wayward Parrots

Devi Jones' Locker:
Packet Trade
Sea Change
Storm Cloud
Floating Point

Fiercely plies the shaft of this my paddle,
Named *Kautu ki te rangi*.
To the heavens raise it, to the skies uplift it.
It guides to the distant horizon,
To the horizon that seems to draw near,
To the horizon that instils fear,
To the horizon that causes dread,
The horizon of unknown power,
Bounded by sacred restrictions.
Along this unknown course,
Our ship must brave the waves below,
Our ship must fight the storms above.
This course must be followed,
By chief and priest and crew,
But place our trust in *Rehua*
And through him we'll reach the land of Light.
O *Rongo-and-Tane*, we raise our offerings.

Sir Peter Buck Te Rangi Hiroa, *The Coming of the Maori*

PART ONE
REVERSE THRUST

These are the end times.

All of us who make this journey—our revered ancestors, our cherished decedents—we are all blessed to be a part of this, the most exciting time for our people since our evolutionary beginnings. It is the nature of humanity to explore. It is the nature of humanity to expand. We are born in tentative steps on two feet. We are born among the stars.

Susanne sat three rows back from Reverend Hue and let his words wash over her. She often didn't exactly pay attention in the service, but she never felt like she was missing anything. She always left those services just as refreshed, just as enlightened as she did those times when she hung on every phrase. Maybe it was the stillness, the ability to just sit and not feel like she had to do anything that was what drew her to the services. Whatever it was, she always felt imbued by the spirit of joy when she stepped out of the small meeting room, regardless of the sermon.

She'd explained it to Lila, her teaching partner at the school, that it was simply being present, with the other followers and the Reverend, that was the act of worship for her. Lila had looked skeptical, but she was skeptical of everything to do with Susanne's faith. That was fine. Susanne wasn't out to convert anyone. The object of her adoration required no believers.

Here we are, taking our first steps as a new species. We see a fallen branch, perceive a use for it, make new connections in our brains. We take a step toward our destiny.

Millions of years away, here we are, taking our first steps on a new world, a new home for our species. We take another step toward our destiny. What transpires in between? Nothing more nor less than the wonders and horrors of all that humanity can be.

Here we are, caring for the weakest of us all. Here we are, murdering our neighbours. Here we are, building the first rocket to the moon. Here we are, burning villages of children. As it has happened, so it happens now and will happen always. We can never be free from history. We can choose only the manner in which we shall play our parts.

Susanne floated weightless in the spherical padded room in the centre of the ship. She hugged her knees to her chest, as compact a ball as she could be. She didn't cry, but she felt like she might. She was seventeen and had just received the notice from the Academy that she'd been accepted into academic training. It was everything she'd hoped for.

But when she saw the notice, her mother hugging her, saying, "I'm so proud of you, honey," Susanne had felt her heart drop. How had she ever thought she could do this? Teaching other people? When she couldn't even understand a simple poem?

It had been years since she'd failed that literature class, so long that the Academy hadn't even considered it in their assessment. But Susanne remembered: she had failed. Images of the exam questions burned the inside of her eyelids as she floated, the word *Failure* ringing in her ears. Even if no one else knew, she always would remember.

"Don't you feel a bit—" Lila asked one lunch break, "naïve?"

"What do you mean?" Susanne asked.

"You know," Lila said, looking sheepish but determined, "gods. Religion. It's all a bit—backward, don't you think?"

"I don't worship gods," Susanne said, a smile growing on her face. "And as for religion, I don't know. I guess you could call it that. From what I've read about them, I thought religions were about controlling people, making them conform to some code. There's nothing like that at our services. It's about how we relate to reality, not what we do in it."

Lila frowned. "If it doesn't tell you how to behave, then what's it for?"

"I guess it's like some of the more esoteric branches of philosophy. Epistemology, maybe, or theoretical physics. We're thinking about the fundamental nature of reality and our place in it." She picked up her sandwich. "None of those things dictate whether I eat this now or save it for later, but they still inform my understanding of the universe."

Lila narrowed her eyes. She and Susanne had taught together for nearly a decade and Susanne appreciated her colleague's attempt to reconcile her faith with her analytical mind. "Okay," Lila said. "I'll concede that it's not certain that you've been brainwashed. For now."

"Phew," Susanne drew her hand across her forehead exaggeratedly. "Now, can we talk about what we're going to do about helping Min to understand linear algebra?"

It is the dawn of a new age. It is always the dawn of a new age. Every second redraws the past into a new shape. It is always armageddon for history. These are the end times. This is the new age. Every moment, every breath, is the first and is the last. There is no beginning and no ending. Only that which we perceive. But our senses are limited and distorted. Our eyes capture the view we see upside down and our brains have to correct the image. We adjust to make prefect sense of our imperfect senses.

We remember something, we call it past. We imagine something to come, we call it future. But what is now? Now can never be described, can never be held, because there is no now. There is no past, no future, no time. No time but all time.

She was certain he was staring at her. Not just him, but the entire class. She could feel their eyes on her skin, their mockery palpable in the small room. When Susanne found the courage to look up from her tablet, she saw only a classroom full of her fellow students looking forward at their lecturer, but she was sure that moments earlier they'd all been looking at her.

She was such a fool. Of course, Malik Ahmed was attractive; anyone with eyes could see that. And that voice—it was like it reached deep inside her every time he spoke. That she ever thought she'd have a chance with him was patently ridiculous. She could feel the sweat pooling in her armpits, just as it had all those months previously when she'd asked him to go with her to the revival of Rich Ibarra's final play, *Sunspots*. And when he'd agreed, she must have looked so absurd with her stupid grin. How could she not have known?

But he'd met her at the play and they'd both enjoyed it; she blathered on about how much she loved *Sunspots*, that Ibarra was the only contemporary playwright whose work she felt she understood. Even as she talked she knew she was making a fool of herself, but Malik suggested a drink afterwards and Susanne felt her stomach flip. She'd felt like the hero of a love story, as if something portentous and magical were happening as they found a small table in a dark corner of the pub. And then he'd been funny and charming as they talked about the play and she was laughing and barely hearing him talk as she concocted a scheme to get rid of her roommate for an evening then— It was as if the ship stopped spinning for a moment, when her distracted ear picked up the words. *My boyfriend.*

"He hates theatre. I was so glad you asked me. Who wants to go alone; the best part is talking about it afterward, don't you think?"

Something inside Susanne broke when he put his hand on hers, saying, "When you're in a relationship, it's easy to forget how important it is to have other friends."

She knew it must have shown on her face—the disappointment, her breaking heart. She forced a smile and agreed, then went back to talking about the play. But he had to have known. Had to have later told everyone he knew, laughing at her desire, her blindness. She wanted to crawl out an airlock.

She'd managed to stop thinking about it. Not forget, of course, but not dwell on it either. Until she'd walked into the new class and there he was. Smiling at her as if nothing ever happened, but her shame and embarrassment covered her like a smothering blanket.

"I know you're tired of talking about it," Lila said, "but I can't help it. I'm curious. If you hadn't mentioned it, I'd never have guessed that you were an adherent."

"It's okay," Susanne said. "I'm not ashamed or anything."

"I know." Lila managed to look embarrassed. "So, did you grow up with these ideas. Your mother, was she a believer?"

Susanne laughed. "Not at all. She still thinks I'm just a little bit crazy. Really, there's nothing you can say about this that she hasn't already said, and then some. No, I came across these ideas when I was studying. I was working on ship's history, some of the less pleasant parts. The bad decisions, the unfair practices. I read a few references to this belief system and I was intrigued. I couldn't stop thinking about it and everything I read made me want to know more. I discovered that the ideas never died out, that there were some small pockets of adherents still. So I went to a service."

"You knew you believed just by reading about it?"

"Of course not," Susanne said. "I was just curious. Kind of like you, I guess." She smiled at her friend, whose face reddened slightly. "At first it was just research, but I met some of the people, made some friends. So I kept going. Then I found that I liked the feeling of having a half-hour where you could be still, where you could be quiet and just think about things. I liked spending time with other people who were interested in these ideas. And it doesn't hurt that the reverend has a spectacular speaking voice."

Lila grinned. "You are a sucker for nice voices."

Susanne nodded. "I can't deny that the delivery is enjoyable. But in the end it's the message that keeps me coming back. After all, Reverend Hue is part of the Portside Theatre troupe. If I just wanted to listen to him talk, I could go to a play."

This is the beginning of a journey. We are almost at our destination. It is a never-ending journey. Many of us feel, in our everyday moments, like there is among us some great sense of completeness, a conclusion, an accomplishment. That we are in the midst of finishing a grand endeavour, and that while we will not see the fruits of our struggles, our grandchildren will be as the heroes of history are to us—the pioneers of a new world, a new future for humanity.

For some of us, this gives us a feeling of pride in our accomplishments, a sense of closure to a mission undertaken generations ago. But for some, it is a difficult thing to know that a goal we and our forebears worked and sacrificed for is so close yet unattainable for us personally. For others, the very real future of change is frightening. We imagine failure-state scenarios, we worry that our lives and those of so many others may have been spent in service of a futile mission. After all, the hard part of flying is landing.

To all of us who cannot help but dream of the end of this journey, whether that dream is a joy or a nightmare, I invite you to join with me in quiet contemplation. I invite you to imagine physical reality as words in a sentence. Each word is complete, the letters are all there. When we read, we provide the sequence, we feel that one. word. comes. before. the. next. But all those words, all those letters, are in there in the sentence. They exist always. It is only us, our act of reading, which makes them become ordered, which makes them sequential.

In this story, our reading is like time. Time which moves though our reality, imposing order. Here we are, in this service, in year eight hundred and forty-three of the White Cloud. *And here we are, building our first raft to journey across an ocean into a new unknown future. And here we are, expanding across the planet of new Earth, making it into a home for us and our descendants. Here we are—in the past. Here we are—in the future. Here we are. Always. We are here.*

Susanne's attention came back to Reverend Hue's words. It had been a few weeks since Lila had last asked her about her beliefs. For a while Susanne had thought that she might come to a service, maybe even join the community. But Lila had stopped asking and Susanne guessed the moment passed, and that something else caught Lila's seemingly insatiable curiosity. It didn't matter.

Her mind caught on the words she'd thought—the moment passed. That was the point of it all, wasn't it? The moment never passes, not really. For so much of her life Susanne always felt trapped by history—not just the academic history of humanity, but also the personal history of her own life—as if past events were brambles which could attach themselves to your leg and never let go. Her memories, her hopes, they always seemed to walk beside her, their influence often stronger than anything tangible.

It was her great weakness, the aspect of her personality which pained her and nearly made her give up on herself. Her obsession with things gone by, with an imagined future. So, as soon as she read about the idea that everything exists outside of time, it profoundly resonated with her. Time as we see it is an illusion—our senses are flawed.

The last time they'd talked about it, Lila had asked her if it was like believing that everything was pre-destined. That if everything already exists, then there is no free will.

"It's actually the opposite of fate," she'd answered. "We like to think that our past made us what we are, that who I am today is the sum of my experiences up to now. But if we believe that our past exists simultaneously with our present and our future, then in every moment we are creating ourselves originally. If we are a point, then we are free."

"There really are aliens out there."

She was drunk, of course; they both were. It was the usual workweek-ending routine of several rounds at the bar before weaving back to their respective quarters and sleeping it off. People had been blowing off steam like this for thousands of years. It was a tradition, Janey thought. Maybe even a ritual. She looked at Tamar over the rim of her glass and grinned.

"Little green men in flying saucers," she said. "Are they going to board us and perform horrific experiments on us?"

Tamar rolled her eyes. "No, they don't fly around in saucers abducting people. I mean, there's no evidence that that's what they do, so there's no reason to think they do. I mean, we don't do that, why would they?"

"Coz they're aliens," Janey said. "That's what aliens do in all the popular stories."

"Since when do literature teachers watch popular stories?" Janey snorted and signalled the bartender for a refill. She looked over at her friend, but Tamar ignored her unspoken question. "You think I'm shitting you."

Janey laughed. "I think you're shit*faced*." She ordered them both another round anyway.

"Well, yeah," Tamar said, "but this is real." She stopped talking when the bartender arrived with two more cocktails. She took a sip, then shifted her chair closer to Janey's. "I know it sounds crazy, but it's true," she said, her voice low. "As far as we can tell, there have never been visitors from other worlds to Earth, and we certainly haven't run into them on our voyage. But they talk to us, after a fashion. They write their messages in the stars."

Janey recognized a look in her friend's eyes, the desperately serious look of the utterly convinced. The drank in silence for a moment, and Janey wondered what this was all about. Tamar did work in the astrophysics lab. If anyone was going to find alien communications out there, it might as well be her. Still, this seemed so... improbable. She wished Lila were there. The newest member of the faculty was a mathematician, just out of the Academy. She could have calculated the odds. Janey eyed her half-empty drink. Or was it half-full?

"I dunno," she said, more to herself, but Tamar grabbed her arm making her jump.

"Come on," the other woman said, carefully standing up from their table at the bar. "Let's go to the lab. I'll show you."

"I don't think this is such a good idea."

"Sure it is," Tamar said, "we can't hurt anything. And I have to show someone, it's driving me crazy not talking about it."

"Wait a minute." Janey stopped walking down the quiet corridor and grabbed Tamar's hand. "Is this supposed to be a secret? Are you going to get in trouble for this?"

Tamar shrugged. "*Secret* is going too far. But they don't want to tell everyone about it for... well, you'll see." She turned to walk toward the lift but Janey stopped her.

"Are you going to get in trouble for showing me this?" Janey asked again, forcing Tamar to look at her. She expected her friend to brush her off, but Tamar paused as if thinking her answer through.

"It's not impossible," she conceded. "But it's worth it. Come on." She turned and, this time, Janey followed.

"I don't understand what I'm looking at." It was pretty enough, the brightly coloured squiggles on the dark background of the screen, but she couldn't find any meaning in the patterns.

"Neither did we, at first," Tamar said, sliding a control pad out of a slot in the console. "But look at this." Her fingers flew across the keys and the waveforms resolved into words on the screen.

Along the reef beyond our shores lies the first way station to the stars. The passage is dangerous but the reward is great.

Janey gasped. "What is this?"

Tamar grinned, the reflected light from the screen illuminating her face. "It's a story," she said, "hidden among the stars, from long ago and far away."

"And you're sure this isn't just from Earth?" Janey asked, her eyes wide as they tracked across the screen.

"Definitely. It's old, like way before humanity old. Plus it's from the wrong direction." Tamar leaned back, her smug grin illuminated by the patterns on the screen.

"Okay, smartass," Janey said, "so, how old is this?"

Tamar's smile melted. "These stories are hundreds of millions of years old. The people who've sent them are gone; their entire civilization is long dead."

"But didn't you say they only appeared a few generations ago?"

"Sure," Tamar said, "but that's the sad reality of the nature of spacetime. These signals are coming from a long way off. A really long way off. They maybe took an eon to reach us, that's just the way of the universe. These are voices from history, but not our history. For us, the stories they tell are like visions of the future."

"So, what's going to happen now?"

Tamar shrugged. "The rest of the team will fight for a while. Some of them are afraid that making this public will cause a panic—things didn't really work out for our friends beyond the stars, and you know how some people are convinced that anything that reminds us of our mortality will make people riot."

Janey nodded. "As if they are the only people competent to understand reality." She sighed. "It will get out anyway, no matter what they decide."

Tamar nodded. "And the folks who want to hide it are in the minority anyway. I'm guessing that by the next generation these stories will be taught in your literature classes. Not to mention what we can do with the technology for decoding them. It was so clever, so elegant: hiding their messages among the stars, in the radiation of starlight. Of course, we assume it wasn't meant to be a cypher, but the data just happens to be invisible to the human eye. To them, we guess, it would have been like watching theatre in the night sky."

"That must have been incredible."

"And it could be again," Tamar said. "That's why I wanted to show you this."

Janey took a deep breath. "It's a big responsibility, Tamar. I don't know if I'm up for it. I'm just a teacher, not even the best literature teacher. Who am I to judge—"

Tamar laughed. "You're getting sober," she said and gestured at the screen. "If not you, who else? You know stories, hell, you love stories. And that's what this is all about—sharing our stories with the universe."

"But it's so..." Janey shook her head, trying to visualize creatures—no, people on some far away planet some hundred of thousands of years in the future, watching the tales of humanity play out before them. "It's so big."

Tamar shrugged and gestured at the screen. "You're right—this is the single most important discovery humanity has made since we've been on this voyage, maybe even in the thousand years before that. And what is it? A glorified pilot chart. Even I can tell that as a narrative it's nothing special. But it was important to them. Important enough that they felt compelled to share it. And now we get a glimpse into another world, another life, if only one part of it. Never forget that what's mundane to one person is exotic to another. Come on, we've got work to do. You've got to pick your favourite stories and I have to figure out this encoding scheme. It's time to put our own messages in the stars."

She stared into the darkness. She could see the light of distant stars, their winking glow a glimpse into millennia past. Thermonuclear reactions long dead, the light reaching across the gulf of space and time to reach her eyes now. No wonder no one ever comes here, she thought. Who wants to look at death?

Lauren Ibarra stood at the porthole in the observation room, the palms of her hands pressed to the clear glass. It wasn't really glass, she knew that, glass could never withstand the crushing vacuum outside, or the stress of the initial thrust all those centuries ago. She didn't know what it was made of, some engineered construct deemed sufficiently space age once upon a time. Doubtlessly, there was a better material available now. Something that didn't warp the view so much, something that didn't hold her fingerprints so well, something not so cold.

It didn't matter, though. It wasn't as if this was the kind of thing which would be replaced. If this window developed a problem, it would simply be welded over, she was sure. In all the years she had been coming to the observation room, she had never seen another person in the place. The glass held years worth of her fingerprints alone.

Lauren had turned sixty-seven the previous day. Not yet an old woman, but no longer young either. In between. Neither here nor there. Just like everyone on this godforsaken ship.

She walked out of the observation room, down the corridor back toward her quarters. She dreaded returning—her son Rich and his partner Dianne would be there, along with Katie. Oh, Katie. Lauren had loved her once, she was sure she really had. But now...

She reached the door of their quarters and could hear the sound of voices from inside. She took a breath, stalling. She knew she would be fine once she got in there, but the gulf between solitude and the company of others was so great. Zero to one is the hardest step, she reminded herself. She moved to stand in the beam of the scanner and felt a moment of panic well up in her as she heard the click of the door beginning to open. Every molecule in her body wanted to turn and walk away. Every muscle tensed, ready to flee.

"Look who's here," a jovial voice called as the door opened and Lauren's fear reached its crescendo. Then, as it always did, the wave receded and she felt a smile—almost genuine—spread across her face.

"Ritchie," she said, stepping into the room and walking into his embrace. "It's good to see you." They hugged briefly and Lauren saw Dianne over her son's shoulder. "And you, how have you been, Di?"

"Really great, Lauren," she said, waiting as mother and son disentangled, then stepping forward for a one-armed hug. "Happy birthday."

"Well, thank you," Lauren said. "Having you both here is the best gift I could ask for. Come on, now, tell me all about the excitement over in Orange Sector. What's the weather like over there?"

The younger couple laughed dutifully at Lauren's poor joke, then began to talk about their lives. "My mentor at the school, Harald Watanabe, just retired," Dianne said, shaking her head. "He's such a force of nature, so dedicated, it's hard to imagine the place without him."

"Hmm," Lauren nodded, wondering what that would be like— retirement. No longer even pretending that you were useful. She kept the thought to herself, letting the kids get on with their news.

Work, plans, children. The same things Lauren herself talked about her whole life, the same things everyone she'd ever met talked about. She smiled and nodded and asked the appropriate questions, waiting patiently for the visit to end.

Lauren knew that she wasn't fooling Katie. Her partner knew she was just putting on a show for the kids. She'd confronted her once, back when they cared enough to fight. "You're lucky that Rich loves you so much," she'd said after one of the annual visits, "that he's blind to your act. But it's disgraceful, Lo, how little of a damn you give about those two."

"I do love them," she'd said, defending herself.

"I know," Katie had said, "but you don't care about them." She'd walked off then, Lauren never knew where. Another thing she didn't care about, she guessed. She knew that Katie's accusation should hurt, that her son's goals and his partner's career should mean something to her. But knowing how things ought to be and making them be that way were two separate things. She'd let Katie go, found a mindless story to watch, and killed another evening on nothing.

By now, Katie didn't bother to reprimand Lauren any more. Lauren sometimes found it funny that Katie had been afflicted by the same apathy that she'd so despised in Lauren. Not the kind of funny that made her laugh.

Lauren knew that she hadn't always been this way. She had been a regular person, just like Rich, once. She'd had hopes and dreams and loves and plans, like anyone else. And she knew that the saddest thing of all was that her dreams hadn't died because they remained unfulfilled. This feeling of emptiness wasn't because of everything she hadn't done. It was because there was nothing left to do.

The next day she sat at her desk, computing soil densities. It was important work and she was very good at it. She'd even enjoyed it once. I feed the ship, she used to say. Not bad for someone who can't even boil water. She'd laughed at her own jokes then, full of a sense that it all mattered, even if she could never have articulated that. Now, it was just activity to pass the time. She knew intellectually that it was still vital work. It just didn't mean anything to her. She could have been doing anything. Digging ditches and then filling them in again. Painting the hull. It was just something to do.

Had she lived generations ago, some well-meaning soul might have tried to convince her to allow her personality and memories to be recorded. She would have refused, of course, but had it happened anyway, someone accessing the construct might imagine that there was some terrible secret which ate at Lauren. Some item of personal history which after lengthy conversation, some building of rapport, would be finally revealed.

But the truth was that there was no one moment, no great tragedy or torment which caused Lauren to lose connection. It just happened. She pictured her emotional life as some kind of gas in a container, a container with a pinhole leak. As the years passed, the pressure difference sucked infinitesimal amounts from the container, so little at a time that it wasn't even noticeable. But the reduction was constant and one day the container that once held her love and admiration, her goals and aspirations, was nothing more that an empty flask with a hole in it.

Does this happen to everyone, she wondered. She looked around the task room at the other senior technicians. There were a half dozen people around her age, the silver badge of authority and experience on their collars. It was a tableau right out of an Academy recruiting holo, people working hard to ensure the successful delivery of a future generation of humanity to a future planetary home. Serious work.

Were they all faking it, too? Had their containers run out of gas, just as hers had? Was it an inevitable result of having outlived one's dreams?

"That's such wonderful news, Pete." Lauren heard Maureen's voice from the break room and the strident tones brought her out of her thoughts. Maureen had always been loud, Lauren thought, but she'd not found her colleague's voice so distracting until recently. Lauren shook her head. Everything annoyed her lately, if she noticed it at all. Still, Maureen's voice had now caused her to notice the time and her own rumbling stomach.

She pushed away from her desk and stood. Something twinged in her right hip and her left knee was stiff. She sighed. She worked the kinks out then walked into the break room. "Lauren," Peter said as she entered, his smile reaching all the way up his face. "Have you heard?"

Lauren shook her head but didn't pause on her way to the cooler. "Danica is pregnant," he said to her turned back.

Danica, Lauren thought. Who is that again? "That's great, Pete," she said, still not placing the name. "You must be thrilled."

"Absolutely," he said, "from what I can tell, the only thing better than being a dad is being a granddad." That's right, she was his daughter. Lauren pulled a salad from the cooler, checking that her name was on the container's lid. She plastered a smile on her face and turned.

"You're going to make a great doting grandfather, I'm sure," she said and patted him on his shoulder. He smiled and touched her hand briefly. Lauren felt something like shame creep up from her stomach, but it dissipated.

"You must be getting anxious yourself," Maureen said. "It's about time for Richard and—what's his partner's name again?"

"Dianne."

"That's right," Maureen said, her voice making Lauren's ears hurt, "Dianne. She must be preparing for pregnancy about now."

Lauren shrugged. "I try not to meddle," she said, raising an eyebrow slightly.

"You're such a good mother," Maureen said, with no trace of irony. "Me, I can't stop sticking my nose in every few days. Of course, I had a boy, so it's no guarantee for me." She sighed. "Still, I can't help but hope he'll end up like Pete, here."

Peter shrugged. "Everyone makes their own choices," he said, "but I couldn't imagine my life without Dan and Beryl. I like my work, don't get me wrong, but when the kids were small I'd have never left home if I could have gotten away with it. You know what I'm talking about, right Lauren?"

He smiled and Lauren felt ice in her stomach. She managed a return smile then stepped to the door of the break room. "I'd better get back," she said and fled to her desk.

She ate her lunch sitting at her desk, the picture of the dedicated scientist. However, she merely preferred the solitude of mathematics and reports to the calculated lies she told whenever she had to interact with other people. *How did it get this bad?* She knew she had once been capable of relating to others honestly. She was sure.

She remembered the dream she'd had the previous night. She was in the quarters she'd shared with her mother as a child, the room seeming spacious as it had when she was small. In her dream, she sat on the bed in her corner of the room, a tablet on her lap. Its screen was covered with an image of space, not the scene she had viewed from the observation room, but something out of a picture story or art magazine—stars twinkling in clusters, nebulae bursting with colour, comets with icy hot tails. She reached out with a child's hand to touch the screen, but it was not solid as she expected. Her fingers disappeared into the void left by the ersatz screen's portal, but she was not afraid. Her fingertips tingled and her dream mind knew that it was the touch of the future, the feeling of destiny being revealed.

She pulled her hand away from the tablet and stared at her fingers. They looked no different, but she could feel something remaining, a shadow of a memory of a powerful sense of home. She looked around her at the familiar room—her mother's medical lab uniform hanging on a peg next to the washroom door, her rag doll Pippa lying next to her pillow, her bowl with its tiny but thriving geranium. She was filled with a sense of contentment, of belonging and of hope.

Lauren's stomach clenched at the memory. She'd awoken this morning, the tips of her fingers tingling ever so slightly and the emotions of the dream still alive in her mind. It had come over her in a wave, the homesickness, the crushing grief over the fact that it had been merely a dream. A dream that had been murdered by her own act of awakening.

She felt her breath catch in her throat and fought to banish the memory. She was too old to wallow in nostalgia. Everyone wants to recapture their youth, it is the mortification of the old. She knew that and had always told herself that she would age with dignity. No desperate attempts to remain youthful for her. But she couldn't help but remember the dream, so vivid, of her own younger self. So open to life. So eager to play her part in the great journey. So ignorant of the banality of life.

Lauren pushed away from her desk, her empty lunch container in one hand. She looked over her shoulder and saw that the break room was empty, so she stood and walked over to the sink. She rinsed her container, watching the swirl of oil mixed in water as it sluiced down the recycler intake, tiny specks of green and red following the flow. It reminded her of those nebulae she had never seen. How very much there was that she had never seen. She had been born on the ship, would die on the ship, never having left the ship. It seemed such a small life.

When the water ran clear, she closed the faucet, dried her container and walked back to her desk. She tried very hard not to think about anything for the rest of the afternoon.

Katie was home when Lauren returned to her quarters. She was surprised; Katie almost always worked late. "Is everything all right?" Lauren asked, dropping her tablet on the small table by the door.

"Everything's fine," Katie said, "I just thought it would be nice to have a quiet evening. Besides, it's obvious the plant doesn't need me like they used to. It occurred to me that I really don't need to be there ten hours a day. I've decided it's time to start slowing down, enjoying life a little."

Lauren frowned. What would she do if she didn't have the lab to occupy her days? The thought made her shiver. "So, what do you want to do?" she asked, the question fraught with meaning in her mind.

Katie didn't seem to see the complexity. "I thought I'd just warm up the leftovers from your birthday dinner. Looks like there's a bottle of wine we didn't get through yesterday, too. Sound okay?"

"Sure," Lauren said and sank into her chair. She'd sat at this end of the table since they'd first moved into these quarters when Katie's daughter Emilie was born. Over the years the foam in the seat had conformed to Lauren's body so entirely that she felt just a little bit uncomfortable in any other chair. As much as she found their small quarters a painful reminder of the past—when she felt as if there were a cornucopia of possibilities before her, a potential for her small life to be something important—when she sat in her chair, she felt as if she were in the one most right place in the universe. It made her sad.

Katie brought her a plate of food and set it in front of her. She looked at Lauren and smiled, her eyes crinkling in a way that had once made Lauren ache to reach out and touch Katie's skin. The memory was almost as strong as the real thing, and she fought to keep her hands to herself. "Thanks," she said as Katie sat down across the table, in her own well-worn seat.

They ate, Katie chattering about her day and her plans to visit the arboretum, the flower gardens, the reservoir. Lauren remembered visits they'd made together, drinking in the beauty of those cherished mementoes of their ancestors' lost home.

Aloud, she said, "I don't know. If you've seen one tree, you've seen them all."

Katie's face froze for a second, then she smiled again. "Maybe that's the point," she said. "To bring all the forests with us to new Earth."

Lauren shrugged. "If you say so."

Katie put her fork down and cocked her head at Lauren. "I know what's wrong," she said. "You've got the day after your birthday blues. A case of let-down after all the festivities are over. All that expectation, all that planning, and now it's over."

Lauren looked at the woman who had been her companion for over two decades. Could she really see so deeply into Lauren's soul? Did she simply mean what she said or was this her way of telling her she understood? That she knew that every day was like the day after her birthday, that every day she felt like she was just marking time and waiting for death?

Katie smiled. "Don't worry. At our age birthdays come around ever other day it seems. You'll be stuffed full of cake again before you know it."

"That must be it," Lauren said and, for a brief moment, she felt something.

Harald Watanabe paused in front of the door, a tiny fluttering in his stomach. He felt very much like he did on the first day of class, a room full of fresh faces in front of him, all their expectation rolling toward him like he imagined an ocean wave crashing to shore would do. He supposed that his nervousness was a sign that he loved these visits, just as it was a sign that he still loved teaching. Sadly, many of his colleagues had lost the excitement he still felt faced with a class full of students.

"Every year is just like the last," Tulia would say over glasses of wine after the faculty meetings. She taught mathematics. "The students don't change, we don't change, the material doesn't change. It's an illusion of progress, that's all."

"Come on," Harald argued once, "of course things change. New discoveries, new ideas. All we have is change."

Tulia had snorted. "You're a historian, you know better than that. Let's say that the whole history of human knowledge is contained by a value of x. All these new ideas, this glorious progress we've made, in the entire twenty-five generations born on this ship, can be represented by less than one trillionth of x. Statistically speaking, nothing has changed."

He hadn't argued. He knew she was wrong, knew that there was more to their lives than propagation, but he didn't feel capable of articulating it. It was a sense of faith in their inherent importance that sustained him, rather than any provable measure. He could live with that, but he could never convince anyone else, which saddened him. And drove him down to lower level N again and again to talk to the kahuna.

"Hello, again, Harald," she said, the lines in her dark face crinkling with her smile. "How long has it been since I saw you, my boy?"

"About twenty days," he answered, simultaneously guilty that he'd left her alone for so long and that he couldn't seem to stay away.

As if she could sense his ambivalence, she said, "The time just disappears, doesn't it? But it is so nice when you visit; I do love our talks together. So tell me, how are your pupils? Eager to drink from the cup of knowledge, I trust."

Harald smiled again. "Oh, Iona," he said. "Were people really so noble in your day? My students barely care where we're going, let alone where we came from. It's a chore to get them away from their stories and music long enough to pass the basic exams. Maybe I was just born at the wrong time."

Her raucous laugh startled him and he saw her wipe an invisible tear from one eye. "Oh, Harald, people have always been that way, especially young people. My goodness, at that age it's amazing they can keep their hands to themselves and their clothes on long enough to go to class. You were probably the same, you just don't remember it. I was certainly like that." Her eyes twinkled and Harald's face flushed. "It will pass, the ideas will get into their brains. I believe in you, my boy. Tens of thousands of years of human history aren't going to disappear from our consciousness on your watch, I'm sure of it."

"I'm sure you're right, Iona," he said. "I just wish that I could tell if I were making a difference somehow."

"Are you losing faith, my boy?"

"No," he said, unable to meet her eyes.

"There's no shame in it if you are." Her voice was so soothing, he was almost willing to admit anything.

"No," he repeated. "It's not that. I do believe, but I don't know why."

"And that bothers you?" she asked. "Not being able to explain it?"

"Of course," he said. "I am an academic, a teacher. I may not be a scientist, but I understand science. I hold its discoveries and methods to be above reproach. So, then, how do I reconcile those values with this..." He opened his hands as if the empty space contained the very beliefs he was describing. "This lack of evidence to show that what we do matters? How do I share this hopefulness, this wonder and excitement about our lives with my colleagues, my students when I can point to absolutely nothing to show that it is real?"

Iona let him finish, her thin lips pursed in concentration. He knew she had heard this all before, knew she'd heard some variant of it from him more than once. Yet she thought about it carefully, as if no one had ever brought this up to her before. He wondered if this capacity for patience was her most supernatural power.

"There are no easy answers to these questions, my boy," she said. "It wouldn't be an article of faith if it were something we could point at with a stick, put in a box and say, 'there it is.' But I know that doesn't help you now. So let me see if I can think of something that might."

Harald shifted in his seat, and for the first time since he'd arrived, looked around the room. It was small, but there was enough space for several visits to occur simultaneously. Some kind of technology he didn't understand was employed to keep the conversations private, but on other visits he'd seen people gesturing wildly, in argument or deep discussion. It amused him to wonder what they were talking about, and made him wonder what he looked like when he talked with Iona. Today, though, he was the only one visiting a relative, and he was thankful for the privacy.

"Sometimes I think this family is cursed by optimism," she said, "damned to be both inquisitive and empirical, but equally sure in our beliefs. It is a surprisingly uneasy alliance, my boy." She took a breath and Harald recognized the characteristic settling-in that she always did before telling a story. All his life he'd loved her stories; they were as much his reason for these visits as her advice.

"My great-aunt Ella was just like you, you know. She wasn't a teacher, but she was a scientist. An engineer, to be specific. Oh, she loved her work. Building things, making systems better, it was all she ever wanted to do. But, you know how it is on this ship—it is a finite space. There is only so much innovation we can sustain, only so much progress we can achieve. It made her a little crazy, I think. She started to think that if there were only some way to tap into the cycle of time, that each of us could do so much more if we weren't constrained by a single life or the linearity of time. It was a wild theory, of course. At first, she kept it to herself, working on her ideas on her own. But soon, her odd questions and strange research became impossible to ignore. When she finally told her colleagues what she was planning, they called the medics. She was determined to be anti-social, unresponsive to medication. She never left the medical facility again."

Harald thought he had heard all of Iona's stories by now, including the one about her ancestor and her brilliant invention but this story had never ended with medics before. "Are you sure?" he asked. "Her invention worked..."

"Yes, it did," Iona said, her eyes filled with equal measures of pride and sadness. "But she never saw it. Years later, other engineers found her notes and quietly finished the project. When the first instance was installed, the Academy called an emergency meeting of the Engineering and History Faculties to determine what to do. They, of course, still believed that it was an impossible idea."

"But, the machine worked," Harald said.

"It did. Of course, it was too late for my great-aunt to see her years of work come to life, which is such a shame." She looked at

Harald, now, a steely glint to her eye. "But, my terrible confession is that isn't what makes me sad. What makes me sad is that she spent her life believing in something she couldn't prove, she let herself be locked away and ridiculed rather than give up what she believed in. What makes me sad is that I don't think I will ever have that kind of faith."

Harald could think of nothing to say. That Ella Mikkels was vilified for her work was shocking enough. That people would imprison someone, ruin their life, just to control an unusual idea—he wasn't sure how to take that. But to have learned that Iona, his kahuna, his totem ancestor, thought her own faith was insignificant was nearly impossible to comprehend.

The door swished open, bringing his attention back to the present. "You have given me a lot to think about, Iona," he said.

"That is all I can hope to do, my boy," she answered, the serene smile back on her face. "The rest, as always, is up to you.

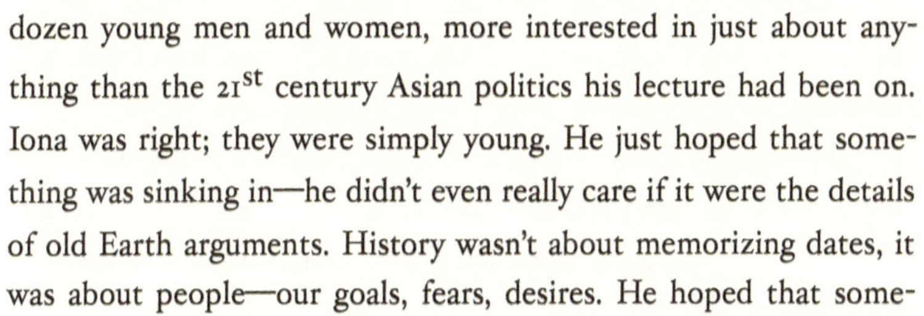

Harald watched his students file out of the small classroom, two dozen young men and women, more interested in just about anything than the 21st century Asian politics his lecture had been on. Iona was right; they were simply young. He just hoped that something was sinking in—he didn't even really care if it were the details of old Earth arguments. History wasn't about memorizing dates, it was about people—our goals, fears, desires. He hoped that something from those old stories would resonate with them, make them see that all of life is a journey, that when one goal is reached another just arises to take its place.

His hand absently fell to his tablet, the touch awakening his place in the text he'd been reading. *Jail-Birds: A History of Incarceration*. Like many features from old Earth's history, Harald would have said that there wasn't an analogue for prisons on the ship. Nationalism, long-distance communication, hunting—there was so much of human life on Earth that just didn't apply now. It was, other than his students' inherent disinterest, the biggest barrier to understanding he felt as a history teacher. It was just so hard to see the connections between the planetary life of the human species and the existence they shared on the ship.

But Iona's reference to Ella Mikkels' confinement in a de facto prison worried him. He didn't want to believe that something like that could really happen, but he was insulated from many parts of ship society. He'd never known anyone who'd had a mental breakdown, who'd acted out in an anti-social manner. He knew intellectually that the medclinics dealt with that sort of problem, but he'd never thought through the implications. Who decides what's pathological and what's merely eccentric?

He checked, but there was nothing in the ship's log. Harald had always been unimpressed with it as a historical reference. He'd given a talk at the annual academic convention a few years back proposing a proper history of the journey, but no one else seemed interested. He'd spent several fevered months after the convention beginning one on his own, but like most of his grand schemes, his enthusiasm had waned long before the project was even outlined.

This was different, though. If the medclinics really were just glorified prisons, even if those days were over, that was major. Harald knew that everyone aboard the ship would want to know the truth. But how to begin?

"So, what seems to be the problem?" Dr. Suli smiled warmly at Harald, who felt like an idiot as his feet dangled like a child's while he sat on the examination bed.

"Uh," he said, "I feel like I'm not concentrating as well as I used to." He shrugged. "Probably just age, but I thought it's worth getting it checked out, right? I mean, that's what you're here for, isn't it?" He swallowed, his mouth dry from the lie. The doctor seemed to believe him, though, and nodded.

"It's not an uncommon problem," she said, "happens to us all." She reached over for a small pad on a wire. "Let's see if there's anything electrical first, shall we?" She stuck the pad to Harald's temple, and he had the irrational fear that he was about to undergo shock treatment or something equally barbaric. "Don't worry," the doctor said, and Harald wondered what he'd done to make her realize that he was afraid, "you won't feel a thing."

She was right. Harald was still waiting for the procedure to begin when Dr. Suli pulled the patch off his skin and shrugged. "Normal. Can you be a bit more specific about these lapses of concentration?"

Harald spent the next ten minutes making up stories that he hoped sounded plausible about daydreaming during class and forgetting to restock the pantry. In the end, he left with the advice to get more sleep and to come back if it got worse, which was fine advice but it wasn't what he'd come for. He hadn't seen any indication that Dr. Suli or any of her colleagues were acting as either guards or police.

As he walked back to his quarters, he wondered if Iona had just been wrong about what happened to her great-aunt. And if she was wrong about that, what else had she been wrong about?

"I'm sorry, but that's really just absurd." Elias Barthes was one of the most even-tempered people Harald knew, and as the head of the Engineering school said the words, Harald saw the other's man's face flush with embarrassment. "I don't mean to be rude..."

"It's fine, Elias," Harald said. "It's fine. The more I looked into it, the more this story seemed—far-fetched. But I had to be sure. Iona..." He looked away, and felt the other man's hand on his arm.

"I understand," he said. "The idea that she could be wrong

about something from the past it's... well, it's almost as disturbing as the story she told you."

"I know," Harald said. "You're certain?"

Elias nodded sadly. "I checked the technical records, just to be sure. Ella Mikkels is the name on the design drawings, all of them. Mark I, Mark II and the final revision that became the system we still use today. It's her signature on the plans. There's just no way she could have been cooped up in some medical facility like a madwoman in the attic."

"Which means there's something wrong with Iona."

Elias nodded again. "And that means there's probably something wrong with all of the ancestor constructs."

Harald stood at the door, his forehead resting against its cool solidity. For the first time in his life, he was afraid to enter the Chamber of the Ancestors. Even as a child, when his mother had brought him to talk with Iona, he'd found the experience comforting. He knew some of his friends were afraid of the kahuna, afraid to talk to the ghostly remains of their long-dead ancestors. But for Harald it was always a cherished gift. That these lucky few people had somehow transcended death, transcended time itself, and through the miraculous technology of Ella Mikkels, were able to share their knowledge with those who came after.

Harald had never understood how the Chamber could have been lost—his great-grandmother's generation rediscovered the room and found that it had been abandoned for centuries. Harald couldn't imagine that people could be so uncurious about their past to manage to forget that the kahuna even existed. It baffled him as much as his childhood friends' discomfort.

But now, Harald began to empathize with the unease his friends had felt. He took a breath and palmed open the door. He saw the communication stations as if for the first time—image screens, input pads, a hard chair to sit on. They could be testing stations for school exams, a console in the most basic quarters. They looked shabby and old, and for a second Harald felt like he might cry. He tried to shake off the feeling and walked over to his usual station.

He slipped onto the stool and entered the code to call up the construct of Iona Kalani. The screen brightened and Iona's face appeared. Harald imagined that he detected a slight look of confusion in her eyes, but told himself he must be imagining it.

Elias had explained that she wouldn't be able to tell that anything was wrong. "It's not like dementia," he'd said, and although Harald hadn't said anything, that was what he'd been thinking. "The ancestor constructs..."

"The kahuna," Harald said.

Elias had looked uncomfortable. "Yes, I understand that's what some people call them."

"It's not some kind of metaphysical hokum," Harald said, "it's a term of respect, for their knowledge, their connection to our past. We don't think they are magical beings or anything like that. But they were chosen by their peers—for their knowledge, for their wisdom. They are, I have to believe, among the best of us."

"I..." Elias said, not meeting Harald's eyes, "I understand that they are important to you, that you learn from them, that you respect their opinions. But," he took a breath, "but regardless of the way the 'kahuna' appear, they are programs, not people. They are like living stories, repositories of knowledge and personality. The construct of Iona is not the same as Iona was in life, not even when it was functioning properly. And now... well, now it's like a bad translation of a dubious source with half the text missing."

"I find that characterization insulting," Harald said, fighting to keep his voice level. "She is not a... bad copy. She may not be human, but she is a person and she deserves to be treated with respect.

They all do."

"I'm sorry," Elias said, "I'm not trying to be insulting. I'm just trying to help you understand the reality here. *Her* reality."

Harald stood and walked to the galley. They'd been at this for nearly an hour and he needed something to do to help him process it all. He rummaged through the cupboards looking for tea and started organizing a snack. He knew Elias was right, at least from the technical perspective. But there was more to it than technical specifications. Sure, Iona was technically just a computer simulation. But what was his own consciousness but a series of electrical impulses? At least she knew what she was. That was more than any human being could ever have claimed.

"Do you think she's in any pain?" he asked as he poured hot water over the leaves, his voice low.

"No," Elias said, and Harald could hear real empathy in the other man's voice. "As far as we can tell, for her nothing will seem any different. Her memories exist only when the program is run, so she has always essentially recreated her whole existence each time she is initialized. She will have no sense that anything is wrong, because from her perspective, nothing is wrong. It's just that her experience is diverging from the human Iona further and further each time she is run. Arguably," Elias said, with a sad smile, "she is becoming more and more her own individual."

Harald looked into those eyes which were so familiar to him and wondered who this was looking back. Her memories no longer corresponded to the woman who had been his ancestor, but her face still widened in a smile of recognition when she saw him. Harald watched the lines on her face deepen with what, a day before, he would have thought of as decades of laughter. Now, they seemed like fissures in time, the markers of an entropy that neither technology nor faith can forestall.

Yet, when Iona smiled at him and said, "Hello, my boy," he found that he just couldn't think of her as a broken program. She was his old friend and confidant, a lifeline to understanding the past which was his greatest joy. Maybe she couldn't provide him with reliable information anymore but Harald knew now that their relationship had never really been about that.

His voice caught in his throat when he answered.

"Hello, kahuna."

He didn't want to be here. He imagined that everyone in the room felt the same way, that they would rather be anywhere else. Fixing the waste recyclers would be better than this detail. But everyone had to take their turn, and this was his. He took a breath and walked toward the body.

Karyl Spencer had never seen a dead body this close before and he sorely wished he weren't seeing one now. It was Su-Ann Miyoki, lying on the table naked, her body a testament to the inexorable flow of time. Karyl hadn't known her well, had probably never spoken to the woman. He was a physicist and she'd been a biologist in her youth—there wasn't much common ground. But she had lived over a hundred years in this corner of the ship and he, too, rarely left the neighbourhood, so their paths had crossed. It never occurred to him that there would come a day when the old woman was no longer walking the paths between the teahouse and the market where she'd sold decorative wreathes.

He kept his focus in the middle distance between himself and the corpse and tried not to think too much. He swallowed hard, but his mouth tasted as if it were full of dust. Dust just like her body would be—no, he couldn't think of that now.

"All right." A strong voice from near the head of the body broke the silence. "Now, I'm sure you all know that your role here is largely ceremonial, but nonetheless vital to the community. You will help me display the body for the witnesses, Su-Ann's kin by heart and blood, and stand by during the service. But, as you know, the most important part of your duties is to come after."

Karyl looked around and saw that the others seemed as uncomfortable as he was. He saw several pale faces and one woman had already sunk to the floor—to avoid fainting, Karyl guessed. "Come," the voice said and Karyl looked up. He still couldn't see the source, having positioned himself as far away from the corpse as possible. "We will run through what is expected of you at the witness ceremony. We can't have any of you fainting then."

The only other funeral Karyl had attended had been for Oliver, his great-grandfather. He was the first person Karyl had known who had died—it happened when he was only twenty-one. Karyl's mother, Johanna, like her mother before her, was not very good with children, so Karyl had spent a lot of his young life with his great-gran. The older man was his favourite of all his kin—maybe it was the age difference, or maybe he was just a sweeter person, but he treated Karyl as if he were a special gift, rather than a necessary burden. He spent as much time with the old man as he could.

When he was little, Oliver had entertained him for hours with tales of wondrous creatures, far away lands and long ago places, with exciting adventures and long lost loves. No matter what else was going on, when Karyl heard his voice, the ship melted away around him and he was transported to another life. One which he liked much better than his own.

When Karyl was fifteen, he went to see Great-Gran in the quarters he shared with his partner, Ellie. "You've always seemed pretty happy," he said over a cup of sweet hot milk with cinnamon. "How do you do it?" he asked.

"Happiness?" Great-Gran asked, one white eyebrow arched. "You're asking me the secret to happiness?" A smile tugged at the corners of his mouth and Karyl felt foolish.

"No," he said, though that was exactly what he'd wanted. "I mean, what's the point? We're all just specks on the timeline of history. Nothing any of us does really matters, not compared to the ones who will come after us. We're insignificant—unimportant." He stared into his cup of milk, watching the thin skin on top wrinkle, flecked with brown from the spice.

"Well," Great-Gran said, "I don't feel insignificant." Karyl shrugged. "There are many ways to be important, my boy," he went on. "Certainly, without us, there would be no ship, no journey, no Earth. We are, in some ways, the most important people who ever lived."

"That's not what I mean," Karyl said, hating the childish whine in his voice.

"Okay," Great-Gran said, ignoring Karyl's tone, "then what do you mean? Think about it before you answer." He stood and busied himself in the small kitchen. Karyl furrowed his brow and tried to think of an answer.

"I guess I mean that I want to be important individually. I want to feel like it matters that I'm me, that I'm not just a walking DNA repository."

Neither of them said anything for a few moments, then Great-Gran turned back to face him. "Well, Karyl, that's up to you," he said. "You are alive in this place at this point in history. You can't control that. But you can control what you do with that life. You can spend your days just going through the motions of a job, doing the minimum of what is necessary to survive. Or you can choose to find something that makes you feel significant."

"Like what?" Karyl asked.

Great-Gran shrugged. "I can't tell you that," he said. "It's one of those things you have to figure out for yourself."

Karyl stared at the wall, thinking. "Did you find something?" he asked.

Great-Gran nodded. "A few things, actually. Love, a family, sharing information and telling stories. When you care deeply about something, it is like rising water in a tub—it elevates everything else."

Karyl nodded. "How do I find it?"

"Just open your heart and mind to new things, be willing to try something strange. One day, if you're lucky, you'll stumble on something that grabs a hold of your mind and won't let go. That's the one."

When Oliver died, Karyl didn't leave his quarters for two days. He cried and slept and tried to pretend that it was all a bad dream, that Great-Gran would walk out of the medical lab all smiles and tell him that everything was going to be okay. But it wasn't going to be okay and he knew it.

He had tried to find that thing that would make him feel special, he really had, but he was starting to wonder if it was just another one of Great-Gran's stories. By the time the funeral happened, Karyl was cried out. As he walked into the Witnessing Room, he felt empty. Not just empty of tears, or pain, but empty of everything, as if he were really a fabrication machine or a cleaning drone, dressed up in human skin. He walked without feeling his legs, spoke to people without understanding the words. He stood between his mother and his grandparents, their eyes red, their hands clutching his, and could barely recognize them. He felt nothing for them, these people who were by definition his family but in reality no different than any other neighbour he saw every few days. With Oliver gone, Karyl was alone. Just another interchangeable part of the biological mass of the ship. Necessary but not unique.

It was the worst moment of his life.

Karyl hadn't thought about Oliver's funeral in years. He also hadn't thought about the existential angst that had filled him in the days between his death and the Witnessing. It was as if in the two days he'd spent mourning his Great-Gran, he'd also mourned the loss of his own hope for individual meaning. When he walked out of the funeral, receiving the condolences of his neighbours with an empty heart, it was as if he'd left all those adolescent thoughts of finding meaning and happiness with Oliver's body, to be obliterated by the flames. As if they, like what remained of his Great-Gran, could be turned to dust and sent to the many communities of the ship, to nourish others as they'd failed to nourish Karyl.

But when the message arrived at his terminal, informing him that it was time for him to fulfil his duty as a distributor, the memory of Great-Gran's smiling face returned unbidden to Karyl's mind. He felt something break in his chest, a hardening that he'd failed to notice, a block between himself and the pain of engagement in the community. It was as if Oliver had died all over again, as if he'd never grieved the loss.

Karyl's roommate, Leanne, came home to find him staring at the screen, the dried salt tracks of tears staining his face.

"Are you all right?" she asked, a stunned look on her face. Karyl had never let his emotions show before.

"I don't know," he answered, turning to face her. "How would I tell?"

During the service, the distributors helped bring in the body, then stood behind it as an honour guard while the Returner conducted the service. They were arranged in a triangle shape, and Karyl's position in the service as the representative of Su-Ann's community, meant he stood at the back of the group. The Returner, the owner of the voice and a man called Charlie, explained that the formation was symbolic of the dead person being surrounded by members of her community, her kin.

"You bind the Witnessing," he'd told Karyl with an air of sincere solemnity, but all Karyl really heard was that he would be furthest away from the body. As he took his place and prepared to suffer through the seemingly endless ceremony, he reminded himself that this was the best he could have hoped for; that once it was over with, he'd never have to do it again.

Karyl heard the sounds of the attendees softly weeping, quiet voices of condolence from around the room as the Returner walked around the body to stand between it and the people who had come to the service. Karyl looked down at his feet, not wanting to hear the words designed to comfort, but that only reminded him of his failure.

He could never explain what it was about the service that so bothered him. He had kept his feelings of unfulfillment so close that he couldn't even describe them to himself, let alone to someone else.

"But, it's an honour," Leanne had said when Karyl finally managed to explain that he'd been called to serve.

"It's morbid," he'd answered, refusing to meet her eyes.

"We're all going to die, Karyl," she'd said, putting the loaf of bread on the table and shuffling the salad over to the side. "It's the way it works. Don't you want your kin to come witness when you go? I do."

"I don't like thinking about it," Karyl said, slicing the bread and spreading hot vegetable sauce on top. "No one would care anyway."

"Come on," Leanne said, "you know that's not true. There are lots of people who care about you—your mother, the other people at the lab... me."

Karyl shrugged and worked to change the subject. "I don't understand why everyone has to be part of this ceremony, anyway. It's not like they need the people—the whole process is practically automated now."

"That's not the point," Leanne said, putting a spoonful of salad on her plate. "It's about making sure that everyone understands what happens when we die. It's about making sure that the communities are connected, that every life is valued."

"It's macabre," Karyl said, "and I don't want to talk about it any more. Let's eat."

Karyl wished that he could have traded places with Leanne. She would have felt the correct amount of solemnity at this moment. She would have paid attention to the meaning behind the words that were intoned by the Returner, rather than just standing there and waiting for it all to be over. Repeating the instructions over and over that the man had given him that morning: One hand on the body, one hand on the next person. Walk to the oven. Pause. Turn. Push. Wait.

Karyl fought not to think about what happened inside the ornately decorated sepulchre. The searing fire, the total destruction of everything that had been Su-Ann. He blinked his eyes and tried to focus on the service.

"Death comes to us all," the deep, solemn voice of the Returner said, the cliché sounding more ominous to Karyl now that it had ever before. "That is certain. All we can do is hope to live long and well, to leave our legacy intact, to give back to the community in life and in death. And so it was and so it will be for Su-Ann. She was a sister, a mother, a neighbour. She gave her life in service to the greatest journey any member of our species has undertaken: to her daughter Penelope, her grandchildren Asta and Chen and her great-grandson Elias; in her work helping to feed her community. And now, as the last gift she will give this community, her dust will be divided and used to nourish the soil in the gardens. As it has always been, as it will always be, life feeds on life. We all live on in each other, we become our own legacy."

Karyl knew it was a lie. Maybe not literally—he knew that the ashes of the dead were used to fertilize the food gardens, and he knew that in a closed system like the ship everything was recycled in some way or another. But it was just the atoms, the constituent parts, which were retained. Everything that made Su-Ann unique, everything that made her human, would be gone with the fires. If there really was anything unique about anyone. He doubted there was.

"I know some of you feel a particular sorrow," the Returner said, "at the death of someone so close to the end of our collective journey. But none of us here will live to see the day when the *White Cloud* reaches new Earth. This is as it has been for our ancestors before us, and just because we can now count the remainder of this journey in decades rather than centuries, we need to remember that we live as our parents and grandparents did, in the knowledge that we have prepared the future. And while we all dream of that moment of humanity's landfall, we know that its splendour is promised only to a few. Our destiny is to ensure that they arrive, healthy and whole, to begin the next phase of humankind. That work is as valuable, as necessary, as the work those first settlers will undertake. And so, as we return Su-Ann Miyoki to the soil of our gardens, remember that her contribution to our mission was no less than that of any other that has been or that will be."

Karyl felt the Returner's words as if they were a blow to his chin. The man was saying what Karyl had feared his whole life to be true, admitting it aloud for everyone in this room to hear. As if it were something to cherish. That no one is special, that the best we can hope for is to leave our remains to the soil, to feed the next generation. Karyl felt tears begin to prick his eyes, and he bit the inside of his cheek to make them stop.

When the Returner had stopped speaking, Karyl felt rather than saw the rest of his group begin to move toward the sepulchre, guiding the body with them. His feet moved as if propelled by some other force, Karyl's own mind unable to do any more than follow the rote instructions he'd been given before the ceremony. One hand on the body, one hand on the next person. Walk to the oven. Pause. Turn. Push. Wait.

He thought he would feel something when he helped push the body into the receptacle, that a sense of horror would overcome him when he heard the whoosh of the fires. But he was numb, just as he had been at Great-Gran's Witnessing.

It was over surprisingly quickly. The dozen small urns of ash were given to the distributors, and each was tasked to return to their communities to share the remains of Su-Ann. So she would be a part of the legacy, the Returner said. As we all will be, he said.

Karyl knew then, knew deep within himself, that he was already dust. Dust made flesh, animated only to work, to eat and sleep and talk, but ultimately nothing more than particles of matter.

The same as everyone else.

Hanne walked into the lab with a pounding headache. She knew something was wrong, knew she should be able to see it, but everything was blocked by the throbbing. How did ancient people manage, she wondered. It was barbaric to have to suffer. She settled on to the couch and laid her head in her arms. Something was definitely wrong.

She took a breath and tried to think. Obviously, she'd gotten contaminated by something. She'd have to get someone to do a complete workup on her—she was in no shape to do it herself. She opened her eyes and winced. Why did they have to keep the place so bright? It was obscene.

She fumbled with her handheld and managed to get the room's lights dimmed to a reasonable level. Then she slowly and methodically poked at the handheld until she found the list of her colleagues. Martine. She would be able to help. She kept similar hours and was familiar enough with Hanne's work that the explanation time would be drastically reduced. She sent Martine a brief message, then gingerly lay down.

"What a strange side effect," Martine said, her bushy eyebrows nearly meeting as she looked at the list of data. She'd isolated the cause of Hanne's pain and, more urgently from Hanne's perspective, relieved it.

"So, essentially this all happened because I don't like the smell of the new compound?" As Hanne's pain faded, her comprehension returned. "But I'm sure there was no odour at all."

Martine nodded. "It's not smell in the sense of a fragrance, but rather the stimulation of the olfactory nerves that caused your headache."

"Hmm," Hanne thought. "So, if I wear a mask I should be able to continue with the experiments."

"I'd think so," Martine said. "Though if it were me, I'd isolate the whole lab. After all, it's improbable that you're the only one with this sensitivity."

"Right," Hanne said, giving her head a shake. "Looks like it's going to take a bit longer to get back to normal than I'd hoped."

Martine smiled and squeezed Hanne's shoulder. "Give it a few hours. So, head exploding spores aside, how is it coming? I'm following your updates, but what's the inside dirt?"

"I think I'm on the verge of something remarkable," Hanne said, unable to keep a grin off her face. "The models are showing that it could be a revolutionary propulsion system. But that's not the really interesting part." She pulled her chair closer to the table and leaned toward Martine. "We could be exploring now," she said. She waited while Martine digested the information and watched her friend and colleague's face change.

"You mean retrofit the ship and make some kind of side trip?"

Hanne shook her head. "No, I mean we can develop smaller ships, tenders I guess you could call them, that we could take out on other trajectories."

"You mean split off other missions."

"I suppose," Hanne said. "I mean, these ships would be much faster than we are. I was assuming people would go out for a short time then rendezvous with *White Cloud* later on, but you're right—there's no reason why they couldn't be one-way trips."

"Huh," Martine said, her eyes narrowing. "This opens up a lot of possibilities."

"I know," Hanne said, grinning. "You can see why I'm excited.

This changes everything."

Hanne sat in her quarters, the lights low, a cup of apple tea at her side. It had been months since the headache, but now she felt something similar. It wasn't a physical pain, but she was reminded of the splitting, nauseating, throbbing headache.

The situation was maddening. She was a scientist, an explorer—she valued the truth above all else. At least, that was what she'd always believed. But now, in the face of these awkward facts, she found herself wishing that she did not know what she knew. She would rather be able to carry on as she always had—for them all to keep living the way they had since the ship launched. The setbacks her own work would have to take in order to address this situation were massive. She didn't even really want to think about it.

But she couldn't condemn future generations to have to live with her refusal to adapt. If she had never done the analysis, never looked further... no, she couldn't think that way. The reality was what it was, whether anyone knew about it or not. She knew they'd all been lucky that she learned the truth in time.

"The calculations are clear," Hanne explained, "we have been losing efficiency on the fuel burn ever since we started deceleration. Actually, it probably began sometime in the initial thrust phase, but it's impossible to accurately extrapolate from that data. My guess is that some debris hit the burners while they were open during thrust and whatever it was put a ding in the jets. It would probably have been too small to register, but large enough to let out that small amount of additional fuel. It's a negligible amount, but over hundreds of years, even a tiny discrepancy from the initial manifest has made a significant impact." She consulted her tablet, even though she knew the numbers off by heart. "If we don't make any changes, we will run out fuel before we arrive at new Earth. By about fifty years."

A hand went up in the small conference room and Hanne nodded at the representative of the Green Sector council. "What about coasting? Can't we just cut the fuel now, then hit the brakes when we get close?"

Hanne shook her head. "We are already decelerating—using the engines to slow us down. The problem with running out of fuel isn't that we won't reach our destination, it's that we can't slow down fast enough to stop once we get there. At the rate we're going, we're going to fly right past new Earth."

The sound of murmuring filled the small room and Hanne waited for the group to quiet down. "This doesn't have to be a crisis," she said when their attention had returned. "I've prepared an initial list of ways we can address this: a scheme to reduce the mass of the ship, a partial retrofit to more efficient engines. And these are just a few ideas I've had. Surely once we all start working on it, there will be even more options." She looked around the table, making eye contact with everyone seated there. "We are going to be fine," she said, "we just have to make it happen."

Hanne couldn't understand it. Was this how decisions had been made back on old Earth? Was the inability to agree on simple solutions to significant problems what caused everything to fall apart? Assuming things had fallen apart—no one really knew why the ancestors had left Earth. Hanne had never understood why better records hadn't been kept; surely the impetus for such a tremendous journey would have been a historical record worth preserving. She'd always assumed that some failure had compromised the records, but now she was starting to understand that the answers to questions like "what happened" and "why did this occur" were not always straightforward.

She was alone in her quarters, looking over a new set of proposals for ways to cut down fuel consumption, when a ping sounded from her console. She sighed. She had only just gotten back to work, after a long discussion with one of the heads of the Engineering school at the Academy—a supporter, thankfully, but the time these discussions took from the real work was maddening.

She looked over at the display and saw an unfamiliar name. She debated with herself—it might be one of the cranks who'd contacted her just to vent about how inconvenient the proposed solutions would be, or it could be something important. She really didn't want to talk to anyone, even if it had been someone she knew to be friendly. But it might be someone with something useful to offer and she couldn't afford to turn any help away.

"Hanne Pukka here," she answered.

"Um, hi," the voice barely registered from the small speaker and Hanne increased the volume. "Ah, my name is Oliver, I'm a technician in the water reclamation plant, but that's not important. Um, I have an idea that you might find useful. I was hoping we could meet?"

"What kind of idea?" Hanne asked. She had heard more than her share of utterly unworkable and completely ridiculous concepts in the previous weeks. She'd become very leery of strangers bearing 'useful suggestions.'

"Well," Oliver said, "aside from the water reclamation plant, I also run a little publication for my local sector. Art and entertainment mostly, a bit of fiction every once in a while, but we also do editorials and news when there's something interesting going on. I don't have anything to say about this fuel situation, but there are plenty of smart people who do. And this is an issue that will affect everyone—I feel like we all ought to to be talking about it."

Hanne frowned. He had a point—the one thing everyone agreed on was that this was a significant issue for the entire population. But so far her experience had been that the more people were involved in the discussion, the further from a resolution they'd gotten. Still...

"I'd be happy to meet," she said, "but I'm afraid that my time isn't what it used to be. Would it be possible for you to come to my lab, in Orange Sector?"

"Absolutely," the voice sounded eager and more self-assured, maybe Hanne guessed, because he hadn't been shot down. "Would tomorrow afternoon be acceptable?"

"I'll expect you," Hanne said and ended the call. She stared at the console, then keyed in the code to mute all incoming transmissions. She leaned back in her chair. She had never wanted anything like this. Not the fuel problem—of course, no one wanted that. But she had never sought attention, never dreamed of being a name that history remembered. She wanted to do useful work, make all their lives better, maybe even create something revolutionary, but it was never about her. She found the attention extremely uncomfortable and somewhat unseemly.

But, like the problem itself, pretending that things were different didn't solve anything. She couldn't avoid being the face of this issue, couldn't stop championing for what she truly believed were necessary changes. Whether she liked it or not, this was going to be her life's work. She picked up her handheld and began reading the new proposals.

"I'd like to have someone write up a brief explanation of your top three solutions, in a format that anyone can understand." Oliver was a slight man, a few decades Hanne's junior. His obvious shyness dissipated quickly once they began to talk about the details of what they might be able to put together for the Green Scene, his public log.

"You're asking for a lot," Hanne said. "This isn't a simple problem and these aren't simple solutions."

"I recognize that," he said, "but there must be a way to make the main issues clear without bogging people down in technicalities. Really, most people just want to know how a particular scheme is going to affect them and whether the inconvenience is worth it. A cost to benefit breakdown."

Hanne frowned. "This isn't exactly my area of expertise," she said.

Oliver smiled. "You don't have to do everything yourself," he said. "I have a friend, Isabel. She's retired now, but she was an agricultural planner. She's good at this kind of analysis and she's interested in getting involved with the log. I think she'd be happy to work on this with you."

Hanne thought about it. "What kind of information would she want?"

Oliver bit his lower lip. "If you get her an overview of each plan, I think she'd be willing to draft something for you to review. You might need to explain some of the more technical elements, unless it's related to plants, in which case I'm sure she'll have it covered."

"This sounds good," Hanne said. "I'm glad you contacted me. I think getting this information out to people will help to create the support we need for these solutions."

Oliver nodded and stood. "I'm just glad that you recognize the value of sharing this information. It's exactly this kind of story that I want in the Green Scene. I'll get Isabel in touch with you right away."

"Great," Hanne said. For the first time since she'd argued with Martine in the canteen, she felt like maybe she was getting somewhere.

... and even the most innocuous of these plans would create significant upheaval for the majority of the population. A reduction in environmental fuel uses would limit the amount or quality of daylight, which research shows can lead to serious mental and emotional trauma. And decreasing agricultural use would result in lower crop yields—in short, much less food for our families.

Hanne threw her handheld to the table, which made a satisfying crash but didn't break. The sensible part of her brain was thankful that her moment of pique hadn't just added to her problems, but the part of her that was just plain angry wanted to break something.

"How could they do this?" she said aloud to her empty lab. "I thought they understood..."

Sadness and betrayal washed over her, the new emotions flooding out her anger. She felt drained. She sank down into her seat and rubbed her temples. She had assumed that when Oliver approached her, it was because he believed in her assessment of the situation and wanted to help. The log was just the means at his disposal. She saw now that it was the other way around—the fuel situation was the story that he needed to make his log more popular, more important. And it had worked perfectly.

The whole ship was glued to Oliver's coverage of the situation. Hanne had to admit that Isabel had done an excellent job distilling her main solutions down to their essence. Unfortunately, he'd gotten another author to do the same with the counterpoint arguments. The special edition did nothing to make the decisions simpler, and everyone was reading it.

The anger came back as quickly as it had gone, hot and rising from her belly. She picked up the discarded handheld and pulled up Oliver's contact. She made the connection without even thinking, then briefly wondered if he'd even bother to answer her call.

"Hanne," he said, his voice light and cheerful, as if nothing had happened. "Wonderful response we've been getting to the piece. You must be thrilled."

"I am not," she said, her hands trembling. "This was not what I understood from our discussions. I— I am having a hard time understanding what you've done here. This information you've provided isn't helping to explain the situation at all. You've included ignorant opinions and fear-mongering alongside a series of facts as if they are the same. This is... this is criminal."

"Now, now," he said, "I think you're not seeing things very clearly. There are at least two sides to every story and I'm just making sure that everyone, every side, gets to be heard. It's my responsibility to give equal time to all the positions here."

"But there aren't two sides," Hanne said, voicing the thought she'd been tamping down since the controversy began, "there's the reality and then there's wishful thinking. This is not the situation I wanted to find myself in, to find all of us in, but I can't just pretend that things are different. Don't you think I'd rather continue as if nothing were wrong? Do you know what I was doing when I discovered this problem? I was on the verge of changing the very foundation of our society. I'd created a way for people to get off this ship, to explore nearby space; in a generation or two we could have possibly sent an advance party to new Earth. It would have been among the most significant engineering achievements that has occurred since we've been aboard. And that's all gone, now. All that work, all that potential. There isn't enough power to finish my prototype, let alone build a fleet. But even if there were, it wouldn't matter because there's obviously no fuel to spare on scout ships and unnecessary explorations. I'd dearly love to go back to what I was doing before, but I can't. I can't pretend that I don't know that there's not enough fuel. I can't pretend that some convenient solution will appear in the future, so I can just go back to living the life I wanted. It doesn't work that way. Not for me, not for anyone. And I just don't understand why everyone can't see that."

She didn't bother waiting for his response. She disconnected the call, turned out the lights in the lab, and went home.

Hanne had to leave her quarters sometime. She was running low on food and it had been days since she'd closed the door, silenced her messages and given up. But the idea of going back out there, amongst the arguing and the anger—it was almost impossible. Just the thought of getting cleaned up and walking outside her quarters made her heart race. She called up the clock on her handheld—01:42, the middle of the night. If she had to leave, now was as good a time as any. Hardly anyone would be out, she could get to the canteen, stock up and probably wouldn't see a soul. It would have to do.

She took a navy shower, her first since her self-imposed exile began. She smiled to herself—at least she was was doing her part in the conservation effort. Not that water reclamation was a significant source of fuel expenditure and she was fairly certain that, with some effort, an alternate source of power could be arranged for that task. Still, at least she was doing something. As she turned the water back on and rinsed, the analytical part of her mind was amused by the fact that she couldn't seem to stop thinking about solutions. Giving up might be harder than she'd thought.

She got dressed and grabbed a canvas bag. She took a deep breath and tried hard not to think about how much she did not want to leave this room. She palmed open the door and stepped out into the hall.

It was dimly lit, part of the ship's day/night simulation. Still, she could easily see her way down the corridor to the common area. She'd read that it was modelled after a town square, but Hanne couldn't imagine something like that in open air. How unsanitary. Various public facilities for the sector were located here—several canteens, shops selling clothes or other items, the theatre and concert hall. Hanne paused at the entrance, knowing that this was where she'd be most likely to run into someone she knew. However, she doubted most of her colleagues would be out after two in the morning.

She slipped into the hall and let out a breath. She couldn't see anyone—doubtlessly there were people around, in the taverns at least—but the main area was clear. She headed directly for the largest canteen, which sold both pre-made meals and raw ingredients. She stepped through the door and saw that the large space was empty of people. She began choosing items and stowing them in her bag, her credit account automatically debiting the cost. She was reaching for a sack of apples when her stomach lurched. She heard the sound of the door opening.

She turned and saw a young man she didn't recognize. He nodded at her, but then turned away and began examining the selection of sandwiches. She decided she had enough and walked toward the door. It was opening when she heard him say, "Hey, aren't you Hanne Puuka? I read about you in the Green Scene."

She wanted to run out the door, but as a child her mother had tried to temper Hanne's solitary inclinations by drilling into her a sense of politeness. Her desire not to be rude fought with her wish to flee and, ultimately, won.

"Yes," she said. "That's me."

He took a step toward her and Hanne clutched her bag of groceries to her chest. "I really wasn't sure about this fuel issue—I'd decided I wasn't even going to vote. But then I heard what you said, that speech they posted, and it really made me think. You made a lot of sense and, personally, I think it's why the measure passed. They're saying it's a combination of things, but if people hadn't heard you getting angry, I don't know if it would have gone the way it did." He cocked his head and looked at her. Hanne didn't know what he was talking about, but what he seemed to be saying sounded positive. "You should be proud," he said, finally. "I think you've done something really amazing here. I'm... I'm really glad I got a chance to meet you."

If she hadn't known better, Hanne would have thought that he had an expression of awe on his face. "Uh, thanks," she stammered. "I better go." She gave him a weak smile and left the canteen. She slipped the bag's strap over her shoulder and hurried back to her quarters. She'd been looking forward to a fresh meal, but now she had a few things to do first. She needed to find out what he'd been talking about.

In the days she'd locked herself in her quarters, there had been a ship-wide vote. She wasn't surprised; there had been talk of asking everyone to decide. Hanne had been opposed to a vote; reality isn't something that can be determined democratically. It didn't matter if the vast majority of people chose to believe that there was no problem—they would still run out of fuel early and be unable to stop. The will of the majority wasn't going to change that.

The vote, however, had overwhelmingly been to enact measures to ensure that the fuel would last. People were, it seemed, willing to give up conveniences and comforts in order to ensure that the mission could be achieved. Hanne felt tears sprout to her eyes. The arguments, the fighting was over. Now the real work could start. She saw the words on her handheld blur and let the tears come. She gave herself a moment.

After, she made a meal and began to think about where to start. She'd have to look at the projects that had been suggested, have to get a list of the people she'd want to work with. There was so much to do. As she planned, something the fellow from the canteen had said rattled through her mind. Something about a speech? She wiped her fingers and picked up her handheld. As much as she was still angry at Oliver, she pulled up the archives of the Green Scene and poked through the recent issues. Her own name caught her eye and she noticed that it was from a few days after the initial article had run. She frowned and punched the link.

Her own voice startled her as a recording began to play from the device. "There aren't two sides," she heard herself say. She sounded so angry, so tired. It was the voice of someone who was fighting for their life and losing. "There's the reality and then there's wishful thinking."

She let it play to the end. He had recorded her, without her permission. Recorded her and then posted the recording on his log. She wanted to get angry, wanted to feel violated. Part of her, she knew, did feel those things, but that part was buried deep for now. Because it had been what people needed to hear. Her personal frustration, her individual fear had been what swayed the vote when real facts and hard data just confused them.

It wasn't the way she wanted to think of her shipmates, of the future of the species. That qualitative emotional pleas were more powerful than quantitative facts. But it had worked. Thankfully, finally, before it was too late, something had worked.

The scent of chlorophyll was overpowering. It made Mark light-headed, the smell of the plants filling his nostrils with their arrogant proclamation of life. He liked the arboretum with its tangle of branches, the mat of greenery, the sound of insects and, of course, the smell of the trees. When he sat among the plants he sometimes liked to imagine that he, too, was a tree, instead of a man.

The particular tree Mark sat under was older than he would ever become. It was constant, nearly immobile, but Mark could see where it had angled itself slightly toward the lights embedded in the ceiling, where its roots had grown over some lump in the soil. It was solid, this tree, but adaptable.

He was so lost in his thoughts that he didn't hear the sound of approaching footsteps. "What are you staring at that old thing for?" the voice said and Mark jumped at the sound. He turned his head then smiled.

"Hi, Mom," he said, patting the seat of the bench next to him. She sat, her movements slower than he'd remembered. He looked at her white hair tied up in a complicated braid, the style the same as she'd worn it when he was a boy, only the colour changed.

"I was just thinking," he said, looking back at the tree which shaded the bench on which they sat, "this tree will still be alive when the *White Cloud* arrives at new Earth. It may even be planted in the new soil." He shook his head. "It's amazing to think about."

"Pfft," Mark's mother said. "It's just a tree. Instead, you should be thinking about children. That's what your legacy on new Earth will be. My descendants will step on the Earth, who cares about some dirty old tree?"

"Mother," Mark said, sighing.

"It's long past time," she said, scowling at Mark.

"I'm not old yet," he said.

"No," she said, "but I am. I want to have some time with my grandchildren before I die, Mark, can't you understand that? I know there are plenty of women who would have you, so don't give me that argument. Stop being so selfish."

He sighed. It was always the same argument, now. He was certain that his mother hadn't always been baby-mad. He was sure that they had gotten along, once. But now. Every conversation was a struggle. He almost dreaded their weekly get-togethers.

When Mark was fifteen, his teacher called his mother into a conference. Mark was sure that he was in trouble for something, but what? He'd called Margarita Osterberg an asshole, but he didn't think she'd ever squeal to the teacher. Not after she'd been the one who started it by punching him in the arm and stealing his brand new paper notebook. Even so, he spent the half hour his mom was at the school sweating and practicing his apology.

So when his mother came home from the meeting, still in her mechanic's coveralls, smiling and humming, he hadn't known what to do. He just sat at the small table which dominated their quarters and waited.

"I had no idea you were so creative," Mark's mother finally said, once she'd poured herself a glass of fruit water and kicked her shoes off. "Siân tells me that you got the best grade on the land vehicle design assignment. She showed me your plans—they were very... original. Siân said they were technically excellent." Mark wondered if this were some elaborate psychological trick to get him to admit to something. His mother was very fond of what she called "giving him enough rope to hang himself." He played it quiet.

"What's wrong with you?" his mother said after a moment.

"Your teacher called me in just to tell me what a good job you did and you don't even have anything to say?"

"Uh," Mark said, "what's there to say? I'm glad she liked my design?"

Mark's mother laughed. "Oh, honey, you are something. Tops in your class, work that's a good couple of years ahead of the rest, Siân said. And you don't even get it." She shook her head and finished her glass of water. "Well, at least you don't have an ego about it." She stood and slotted her glass in the cleaner. "Siân has recommended you for early entrance to the Engineering Academy. You should think about it. It's a great opportunity, but don't feel pressured into anything. You can be anything you want to be—the important thing is that you love your work." She looked at him, looked deep into his eyes. "I know it's a bit rushed, but if you want to go, we have to tell them in four days." She leaned down and kissed Mark's forehead. "I'm proud of you, sweetie. Let me know what you decide." She walked into her bedroom and the door slid shut.

Mark didn't understand what had just happened. He was still half convinced that she would come out of her room, yell "gotcha" and then yell at him for the asshole comment. It took him several minutes to replay the conversation in his mind and finally understand what she was telling him.

The Academy was almost as far away from home as it was possible to get on the ship. Almost all the other students would be boarders as well, since they drew enrolment from the whole population. "Excellence Above All" was the motto and they meant it. When Mark first stepped on to the large campus he could feel an almost physical sense of purpose to the place. He knew that all the ship's engineers were graduates, but also all the head technicians for the medical and food labs, plus the designers who worked on the Landing Project all came from the Academy.

Until he wandered into the Landing Building, Mark had no idea that already there were fully formed designs for landing craft for when the ship reached new Earth. It seemed like that was still so far away; none of them would still be alive when that day arrived. But he learned in his introductory classes that it was never too soon to begin creating prototypes. The longer ideas were made real, the more people could tinker with them and the better the final product would be. It was like evolution, his teacher said. It made Mark think about the trees.

There was a small park on campus, about a tenth the size of the arboretum back in his old neighbourhood. It wasn't the same, but Mark spent more than his share of time on the lush clover of Moana Park. He'd read his texts, work out some mathematical problem, stare at the leaves of the tiny plants. Trying to make his designs as seamless, as robust as the plants. Sometimes, he would find that minutes would pass while he was just staring at the clover, his mind blank as he imagined a plant's mind must be. He loved those moments, though the guilt from wasting time which inevitably followed cancelled most of his enjoyment.

At the term's break, Mark caught the train back to his neighbourhood. The students had twenty days off and Mark went back home. His roommate, Jorge, was going to a resort on the reservoir along with several other first years, but Mark couldn't imagine not going home. He hadn't seen his mother in almost half a year. He had never been away from her this long before.

"Come on," Jorge had said, "come with us. It's going to be great. We've got a hut right next to the reservoir. There's going to be swimming, rowing; Mathilde is bringing that jet boat she built. You'll love it."

"Jorge," Mark said, looking at his feet. "I have to go home."

"No, you don't," Jorge said. "You can do whatever you want. Look, you can always go home next break, but this trip won't come around again. It's now or never."

Mark had just shaken his head. Jorge was already eighteen, already a grown man. The two years between them was a gulf as wide as the reservoir itself but Mark didn't know how to explain it to his roommate. He just said, "I can't," and that was the end of it.

Mark's mother hugged him hard when she met him at the train station. "Tell me everything," she said once she'd let him go. They walked the few hundred metres to their quarters—her quarters, now—and Mark told her about school. He was still talking when they got seated at the table, a pitcher of his favourite fruit water and a tray of nuts and bread in front of them.

"Phew," his mother said when he'd finally run out of steam. "It sounds like you made a good choice. The Academy sounds right up your alley." She grinned and Mark ate a piece of bread. "I'm so happy you found something you love," she said, and Mark thought he saw a shadow cross her face. "You know what they say, if you love your job, you never work a day in your life."

On Graduation Day, Mark looked out over the audience seated on the clover of Moana Park. As if her face was lit specifically, he immediately picked out his mother in among the other families. She smiled as if it were the most wonderful day of her life and Mark felt something grow in his chest. He felt a nudge in his ribs and turned his eyes toward Mathilde, trying not to move his head.

"You see your mom?" she whispered as her fingers wriggled down Mark's side to find his hand.

"Yeah," he whispered back. "You?"

He could feel her nod. He squeezed her hand and grinned. He wished he could squeeze this moment like a fruit, saving the nectar for later. He would take tiny sips each day to taste this feeling of accomplishment, the excitement of new beginnings, the pride in his mother's face. But he knew that this moment would pass like the dying leaves on a tree, to be replaced with new moments, new feelings, new experiences. He knew that this is what it meant to be alive, to have moments come and go, only imperfect memories lingering. He knew, but he wished that he could stop time, just this once. For this one moment, his life was wonderful.

Later, he would remember that day with sadness. The screaming match when Mathilde left him. The nights spent curled up in his small bed, covers pulled over his head, as self-doubt ate at him. He had been a prodigy in school, but he was one of many above-average students at the Academy. He'd done well at the Academy, but he was just another new hire at Planetary Designs, and the rest of his team treated him as if he knew next to nothing. He had to admit, they were right—school taught him a lot, but experience taught more. The people he worked with were stars and he was just the new guy.

In those early years, when he remembered that afternoon on the clover, his mother's pride beaming up at him like the lights in midsummer, he almost wished it had never happened. The promise of success, belied by the reality of life, hurt more than he imagined never having experienced that moment of confidence would have. Is it truly better to have loved and lost, he wondered. Is it?

For a topic that he'd only first learned existed when he began at the Academy, planetary engineering was surprisingly suited to Mark. It was as if it had always been his specialty, he'd just never known until then. He struggled at first—so much was new, and it didn't come easily like his school work always had previously. But the challenge was intoxicating.

It was that challenge, the puzzle of making the machines work in different gravities, in unknown terrains, that kept him going the first few years at PD. Aside from his immediate supervisor, Mark couldn't tell if any of the other engineers in his unit even knew his name. No one was impressed with him any more, which was both demoralizing and liberating. If it kept him under his blankets feeling sorry for himself on his days off, it also freed him to make mistakes, to take risks.

He never talked to his mother about any of this, though. When she would call, he'd put on a smile and tell her everything was fine. He'd talk about the technical aspects of whatever he was working on, and when she asked about friends or relationships, he'd change the subject. He knew she knew what he was doing, but he silently thanked her for never pushing. Not then. Not in the early years.

Is it just something to do with age, he wondered. Once he turned forty, it seemed like everything changed. It couldn't have just happened overnight, could it? It must have been a slow evolution, so slow it wasn't noticeable until you took a step back and realized that your whole life seemed to have changed.

There was no obvious moment when his confidence returned, no *eureka* moment. But as Mark became more skilled at his work, the other engineers began to notice him. At first it was chatting over a problem, then the odd invitation to lunch. Soon there were regular outings to watch the ball games, dinner parties, evenings at the theatre. Friends. Occasional lovers. A life outside work.

And at work, Mark became known for his particular vehicle designs, was even sought after by some of the senior people. When he was asked to speak at the annual Engineering Convention about his theory of suspensionless buoyancy, it didn't even seem strange. But he didn't really notice, still thought of himself as that doubt-ridden young man, until one day shortly after his fortieth birthday, he walked through the arboretum. He looked idly at the trees, ran his hands along the soft needles on one of the branches, and realized that he was happy. And had been happy for some time.

He sat among the trees that day for over an hour, filling his lungs with their smell and his heart with years of ignored joy.

When he got back to his quarters, he called his mother.

"You would not believe the day I've had," she began, before he'd even had a chance to say hello. "There's some kind of corrosion in the starboard pump. It's making the most awful racket. Those noise dampeners they give us don't do squat and I've spent the day lying on my back with my arm up a pipe listening to the pump squeal and groan. I swear, this ship is going to fall apart as soon as it touches down on new Earth, if we're lucky."

"That's too bad," Mark said, taking a breath and trying to figure out how to explain to his mother that he finally understood what success meant to him.

"Too bad?" she said and made that disgusted snorting noise Mark hated. "It's a disgrace. How can they expect us to keep on top of all the maintenance when nothing goes on the jobs list until it's practically broken? This isn't just some inconvenience; the water pumps are part of the core system. Without water there's no food, no sanitation system. How long do you think they'd want to go without fresh food? There's no forethought any more, Mark. I tell you, in my day we wouldn't be waiting until the last minute to do routine maintenance like this. No way."

"Well," Mark said, filled with a sudden desire to defend his generation, "there's a lot of redundancy in the water system. I've seen the specs, we could lose ten of those pumps before there would be a loss to the total system."

"Oh, you think you know everything, don't you?" she said. "Engineers. It must be nice sitting in your clean offices, with your calculators and your drawings, getting your meals delivered while the rest of us actually do the work."

"Mom, please," he said, wishing he'd never told her about the office canteen service. This was not the first time she'd mentioned it, as if eating at your desk were the same as getting a free holiday. "Anyway," he said, trying to stop the downward turn the conversation was taking, "I've got some good news."

"Well, I'm glad to hear it," his mother said, "it'll be nice to hear something positive for a change."

"I've been invited to give a public talk at the Academy," Mark said.

"How exciting, honey. What's it about?"

"Imagined planetary scenarios," Mark said. "I'll be talking about the different kinds of environments we could find on a habitable planet."

His mother made a face, then smiled. "Well, I'm sure that will be fun for you," she said. "I can't imagine there will be many people interested in that topic, though."

Mark shrugged. "It's what they asked me to talk about," he said.

His mother didn't look convinced. "I just think it's a shame you never do one of these talks on something interesting."

"I think it's interesting," he said.

"I know, honey," she said. "I just wish for once you'd talk about something real, not this airy fairy imaginary world business."

A tightness grew in Mark's chest that warned him he might say something he'd later regret. "Well, I'd better get going," he said, forcing a smile. "It was good to talk to you."

"You too, honey," she said. "We should really do this more often."

No, we should not, Mark thought as he ended the call. She hadn't even bothered asking when his talk would be broadcast. Though, at least that way he wouldn't have to be disappointed when her name wasn't on the attendee list.

"There's no point in me signing in, honey," she'd told him when he'd asked her why she hadn't watched his last lecture. "It's just not a subject that interests me."

"Has your mother gotten weird as you get older?" Mark asked Isabel

Nieklewicz. They were in Isabel's quarters, drinking a bottle of wine that cost two days' credits, a beautiful Earth sunset view on the screenwall. Mark barely remembered the first time he'd sat on the settee in Isabel's room, his heart pounding in his chest. They had met at the arboretum, where she worked as a horticulturist. He'd been walking along the path, staring up at the canopy of leaves, and had literally fallen over her. It hadn't taken long until he had fallen for her as well.

That first night in her quarters she had seemed so calm and in control, leading him to the settee and laying her hand on his knee. Later, she told him she was as nervous as he was, but Mark never believed it. It seemed to him that Isabel was never nervous. Confidence was one of the things he loved about her.

"I guess," she answered, her eyebrows contracting as she thought. "Everyone gets kind of funny as they get old, I think."

"Yeah," Mark said. "I mean weird with you."

"Like how?"

"Well, you know how some people never get along with their mothers?" he said, leaning back into the soft cushions and steadying his glass on the side table.

"Sure," Isabel answered.

"Well, not me," Mark said, "my mom and I always got along great. At least, that's what I thought. When I remember being a kid, I remember her being supportive of everything I did, she was like my best friend. She always told me I could do anything, and I believed her. If it weren't for her, I'm sure I never would have had the guts to go to the Academy—I never would have lasted the full five years, that's for sure."

Isabel smiled. "You were lucky," she said. "Lots of kids don't have that kind of support."

"I know," Mark said. "That's why it's so strange."

"What is?"

"The way she is now," Mark said, picking up his glass and taking a long drink of wine. He stared at the colours of the sunset, wondering if it were really true that the refraction of light on the particles in a planet's atmosphere could make such beautiful patterns, or if the image were just some artist's conception of what a sunset should be like.

"It's like she doesn't want to know anything about me anymore," he said, "unless it's something that has to do with her. She doesn't care about anything I do, except to complain that it's not interesting to her. I call her to tell her something great and I can barely get a word in while she makes the same criticisms she's been making for the past three years." He looked down at his hands. "I am sure it wasn't always like this," he said. "Is she just not trying any more? Am I that much of a disappointment?"

Isabel slid her arm over his shoulder. "You couldn't possibly be a disappointment," she said, squeezing him. He shrugged and she squeezed harder.

"I think I know what you mean," she said. "My mom isn't like that, not exactly, but she was never a big booster to begin with. She was always pretty self-centred and that hasn't changed. But her husband Ty has gotten a lot more selfish as he's gotten older."

"Yeah?"

Isabel nodded. "Ty was the one who did things with me and my brother when we were kids," she said. "He was a lot like your mom, actually. But now he just wants to read his stories, watch the ball games and hassle us about grandchildren."

"Ugh," Mark said, slipping out from under Isabel's arm. He still got the cold sweats when the topic of children came up. He knew that Isabel didn't have many years left before she ought to get pregnant. He also knew that he would rather be the baby's father himself than see Isabel use a specimen from the bank. But it still made him feel slightly queasy.

"I know," Isabel said, grabbing the wineskin and filling their glasses. "I have this theory," she said. "You know how they say that really old people are like little kids?"

"Sure."

"Well, I think this is a part of it," she said. "Children believe the entire universe is about them, and I think maybe old people are like that, too. They start forgetting that we're individuals, they only see us as their legacies. We start to exist only as ways for them to live on once they're gone."

"Oh, Isabel," Mark said, "how horrible."

She shrugged. "It's why we all have children," she said, "so humanity can continue. There's nothing surprising about it on a societal level, we shouldn't be so shocked that it's ultimately the same reason people individually have children. To avoid death."

Mark put down his wine glass. "That's depressing, Is."

"It's why I like trees," she said, snuggling into the crook of his arm. "They don't have these problems."

"Maybe that's just because they can't talk," Mark said, but he smiled and pulled Isabel closer to him.

It was an oak tree, Isabel told him. His favourite tree in the whole arboretum, though it make him feel guilty to admit that he had a favourite. He loved the roughness of its bark, the strength of its branches, the funny shape of the leaves. He wondered how many people before him had sat beneath its boughs, telling their secrets, their hopes and fears to its silent arms. What wonderful future might this tree behold, the end of this journey that had consumed Mark's ancestors, had consumed him?

He heard footsteps on the path and turned to look. In the dim light she almost looked as Mark remembered her from his childhood. Tall, solid and strong, her mechanic's muscles hidden under the shapeless clothes she favoured. Her hair, bound up in its braid, her softest feature. He could almost imagine the conversation he could have with the mother of his past—free, open, easy.

"Hi," he said as she approached the bench, the reality of the white hair, wrinkled skin, and slight stoop shattering his fantasy.

"Ooh," she said as she sat. "I'm getting too old for this kind of thing."

"We don't have to meet here," Mark said. "I can always come to your quarters, or call..."

She shook her head. "It's good for me to get out. Doctor Witters says so every time I see her." She snorted. "Though I can't see why I bother; no one ever lived forever by going on a walk every few days." She laughed but Mark thought it didn't seem like she really found anything funny.

"So, what's new in the exciting world of Planetary Vehicles?" she asked.

"It's just work," he said, "same as always."

She nodded. It was what he'd said every time she asked lately and she never questioned it. "The young guy they got to replace me is just unbelievable," she said. "You'd think they don't teach anything in the apprenticeship any more. I got a call from Rowan last week, said this new kid spent half an hour trying to just torque on this seized bolt. Nearly burst a blood vessel, Rowan said," she laughed and Mark smiled. "Finally Rowan couldn't stand it any more, walked over there and gave the wrench a good whack with a mallet. Bang! Bolt turned no problem after that. The kid was so tired out he didn't even know to be embarrassed." She shook her head. "Shameful, I tell you."

"You were are good mechanic," Mark said.

"I know it," she answered, but Mark didn't hear any ego in the statement. "Mechanical is good work," she said, her voice taking on a wistful tone. "Engineering, too," she added. "Making the ship go, getting us where we need to be, that's what we're here for. The rest is just the in-flight movie." She laughed again, still without humour.

"I guess," Mark said.

"Well," his mother said, smoothing her hands on the legs of her coverall, "I'd better get back. Who knows how long it will take on the return trip, my legs aren't what they used to be, no way."

"You want me to walk with you?" Mark asked without thinking.

She looked at him, an eyebrow raised. He thought for a moment that she would take him up on his offer, that this exercise in lies of omission would be prolonged further, but she finally shook her head.

"No," she said. "You've got things to do and I'd just slow you down. And I don't need a babysitter quite yet." She turned to walk down the path. "Talk to you soon, son."

"Sure, Mom," Mark answered and watched her go. Minutes had gone by when he heard a rustling from the other direction. He turned and saw Isabel walk toward him with a sad look on her face, the bulge of her belly noticeable only to those who knew.

"Are you ever going to tell her?" she asked, her hand on her stomach.

Mark shrugged. "What's the point?" he said. "It's not about her." Isabel sat next to him and held his hand. "No one cares who fathers a child, anyway. She'll probably never find out."

"I don't want it to be that way for us," Isabel said. "I want our child to know who their father is, like I did. I loved knowing that Ty was my father, was my brother's father."

Mark looked at her, thinking about the many questions she was silently asking. He thought about the trees, how they drop their acorns and then leave the result to chance. Some grow into new trees, some are eaten, but the parent tree never knows. And those few new trees, born from their own accident of fate, they never have to know that the shadow cast over them comes from the tree which gave them life, to which they owe their very existence. They are free to grow or wither as they will, safe in the knowledge that if they grow tall and strong it is from their own efforts. And if they fail, it will be only their own disappointment.

He wished he could become an oak and watch lovingly from a distance as his own child grew or withered, became strong or brittle, not as a reflection of him but as an individual in their own right. Maybe when he came to finally fall to the loamy floor, he could fall with grace, without thrusting all his fear of annihilation on to those who came after him. It seemed an almost impossible task, yet how could he not try?

He looked at Isabel, the green of the leaves reflected in her eyes, eyes which asked the nearly impossible.

"I'll tell her," he said.

It was a long voyage
It was a hard voyage
But like the bird is drawn to the scent of trees
So too did the people draw nearer to the island in the stars
The land promised them by their ancestors
So near that the eyes of the ship could see it
The nose of the ship could smell it
But the people were blind

As if it were a living creature
The ship guided them

All aboard yearned to know the face of their new home
The land which would embrace their grandchildren's grandchildren
And all who would come after
But this was not for people to know
Not for generations to come

The ship's lifetime was long
The journey nearly over
But people live only for the blink of an eye

As if it were a loving creature
The ship guided them

PART TWO
CRUISING SPEED

It was barely a speck when it first appeared on the screen. Gina squinted, as if that would magnify the image, but all she needed to do was be patient. The speck grew, infinitesimally at first, but soon it was a clear disk in the middle of the void of space. Gina felt something primal inside her as it grew larger, as if it were expanding to fill that emptiness out of a sentient desire to combat entropy.

It didn't take long before Gina could make out shapes and colours in the disk—a sphere, really, but there wasn't even the illusion of depth yet. She watched as it grew larger, drew closer, the blues, greens, whites and browns making patterns that were familiar and foreign at the same time. Closer, she thought. We are getting closer every day.

She paused the replay on her screen and stared at the planet. It was so beautiful, she thought. The most wonderful thing she had ever seen. She must have watched this image a thousand times and it never failed to make her breath catch in her throat. Only recently, though, had she taken to playing it in reverse.

She chose the play forward selector and watched old Earth disappear as she'd seen it do so many times before. She preferred her new tactic of watching the image in reverse, imagining what it would be like to see a new planet heave into view. She would have given anything to be able to still be alive when the ship reached its destination. What was thirty decades? Nothing. Barely even the blink of time on a cosmic scale. But she would not live that long, her children's children would not live that long. Still, it made her smile to know that someday people who walked the same corridors as she did would see a vision not unlike that which she had created for herself, but real. That this voyage would finally end and their destinies would manifest.

Gina heard the sound of the door opening and quickly closed the file. She turned in time to see Devon walk into their quarters. She stood and walked into his warm embrace. "How was your morning?" she asked when he'd withdrawn.

"Good," he said. "Great, actually. There's a prime spot coming free in the market and I've been given first bid."

"That's wonderful," Gina said. "Location matters a lot."

"I know," Devon said, sinking into the soft chair he favoured. "I really think that this might start paying off for us."

Gina sat on the arm of the chair and smoothed Devon's long hair. When they had met it had been black, a shock of darkness against his pale skin. Now it was shot through with silver, but still luxuriously full. "The credits don't matter," she said. "You paint so beautifully that it would be criminal not to share your talents. I don't mind bringing home the credits so long as you don't mind making do with this." She spread her hands out to indicate the small quarters with their spartan furnishings.

"I'd be happy living in an access tube so long as we could be together and I could paint," Devon said, finishing his part of this well-worn conversation, "but hopefully we can do better than this soon. It's about time, Gina, don't you think? About time we had a little luck?"

She kissed his forehead. "About time," she echoed.

Devon spent his mornings at the garden, to catch the good light he said. It was convenient for Gina, because she worked the second shift at the water reclamation plant. Devon's early morning session gave her a few hours on her own each day. A few hours to watch her image, to focus on her own practice. She knew she couldn't tell even Devon, knew what would happen if anyone learned about it. It was her secret, her own private worship. She knew that there were forces in the universe beyond human understanding, and she also knew what would happen if she talked about them. It had happened before. She was careful now.

She was barely a teenager the first time. That was the only reason she got away—she told the people who interviewed her that she didn't understand, that she just did what she was told. They'd believed her and let her go, but she saw what happened to her friends. She saw them taken away to the medclinic, their kin told that they were sick and that they had to be removed from society and helped. She shook her head, fighting the anger that still rose in her when she thought about it.

Even then, part of her died a little when she denied her faith. She knew it was a sin to parrot the false theories they taught in school. But Reverend Sproule was clear—it was a greater sin to be denied the ability to worship than to pretend disbelief. Gina herself heard the reverend claim not to be a member of the outlawed cult when the meeting had been raided. They'd been caught in the act, though, the illegal act of worship. It had been impossible for the others to plausibly deny involvement. Gina knew she had been blessed in her escape.

Of course, she was watched. She was only thirteen, so it had been easy to monitor her. Until she was caught at the meeting, she'd been left more or less to herself. Gina's mother, Barbara, was a senior engineer. She spent far more time away from home than she did in their double-sized quarters, so Gina had the run of the place. Even so, she had a room of her own with a bed and a half dozen of her very own toys. As soon as it was practical, Barbara hired a caregiver for Gina, a young woman from a neighbouring farming community. Zola.

From the beginning, Gina loved Zola with the fierce loyalty of the very young. She would cling to Zola's hand when they walked to the park and Zola would have to coax Gina with promises of treats in order to get her to go play with the other children. It was while Gina was climbing up the rope ladder castle that she first saw Reverend Sproule. Of course, she didn't know who the woman talking with Zola was, she just knew that Zola treated this woman with more respect than Gina had ever seen her free-spirited nanny exhibit.

"Zola, Zola, Zola!" she called from her perch at the top of the ropes. Her beloved face turned away from this newcomer to see Gina waving at her. Gina saw a look she didn't understand cross Zola's face as she waved back at Gina, a look that seemed to hold fear, hope and self-consciousness in equal measure.

She was immediately curious about this person who could make someone as constant and strong as Zola lose her confidence.

"Did you have fun today, little one?" Zola asked as Gina clutched her hand on the walk back to Gina's quarters.

"Uh huh," Gina said, looking up at Zola. She stared at the woman, questions she didn't have the vocabulary to form filling her gaze. Zola stopped around the corner to the entrance to the food market and knelt down before Gina.

"Can you do something for me?" she asked and Gina nodded earnestly. "Can you keep a secret?" Gina nodded again, her lips parting a little in excitement. "The lady I was talking to at the park today, it's important that no one else knows that I was talking to her, okay?"

Gina frowned. "Is she a bad person?"

Zola shook her head and Gina saw a flash of anger in her eyes. "No," she said, "she is definitely not a bad person. But there are people who don't understand that and they want to hurt her. And if she gets hurt, I will be very sad. So, can I trust you not to tell anyone?"

Gina didn't hesitate. "You can count on me," she said. Anyone who was important to Zola was important to her, too. Gina would protect this strange person at any cost.

At first Gina didn't like sharing Zola with Reverend Sproule, who began spending more and more time with them. She missed the days when Zola would spend all day playing with her, reading stories or drawing. Now, Zola still woke her in the morning with warm bread drizzled with honey, then helped her get dressed, but now as many days as not Reverend Sproule would arrive and Gina would be, not ignored, but not the centre of attention. There were times when she thought seriously about breaking her word and telling her mother about Reverend Sproule. She was certain, even though she did not know why, that her mother would be very unhappy if she knew what was going on.

But Gina also guessed that if Reverend Sproule was sent away, Zola might go with her. And she had promised Zola to keep her secret. If she told, Zola would be angry and Gina did not want that. She forced her young, impatient mind to abide.

By the time Gina was about to start her first day at school, she had become almost as fond of Reverend Sproule as she was of Zola. The three of them would spend hours talking about the universe beyond the walls of the ship, about old Earth and their ancestors. Reverend Sproule explained that many people of Earth had believed in creatures of infinite power which had created the universe, the Earth and everything on the planet. She explained that they were called gods and the people worshipped them as if they could affect their everyday lives. Gina had laughed and asked if the people of Earth were stupid.

"Not stupid," Reverend Sproule said, "just ignorant. And when they had science to explain their world, many of them still clung to the old beliefs because the stories were powerful to soothe them. It gave them rules to live by, a community to join. And they knew, deep inside, that to worship that which is greater than yourself is one of the most fundamental parts of humanity."

Gina frowned. "But, did they not have kin? Laws? Why did they need imaginary beings to make their rules?"

"Well," the reverend said, "the beliefs themselves were kind of like those nettles in the gardens—once they attached themselves to someone it was hard to get them off, and people passed them on to their children and grandchildren. You know how those nettles are— long after they've died and can no longer spread their spores, they still hang on to the fabric of your jacket."

Gina nodded, but she wasn't entirely sure she understood the metaphor. "Well, at least no one here believes in imaginary gods."

The reverend and Zola looked at each other and Gina wondered if she had said something wrong. "No," the reverend said. "No one believes in gods. Not like that."

Gina remembered sitting at the large table in her quarters, her tablet in front of her, puzzling over her homework. "Is a parsec bigger or smaller than an Astronomical Unit?"

"Why don't you look up the definition of each?" Zola said and Gina sighed. She wished Zola would just answer the question. It wasn't math homework, she was just trying to understand this poem, *Infinite Stars in a Finite Sky*. She knew there would be a question about it on her literature test. That was how Zola always was, though. Even if she knew the answer, she always made Gina find it herself.

She looked it up and then went back to the poem. *Hope as wide as a parsec*, she wrote in her notes, *is really big*. "I can't even imagine distances that big," she said absently to Zola, trying to stall finishing her homework.

"It is an awesome concept," Zola said, her voice serious, "the vastness of the universe in all its wonder."

"Yeah," Gina said, not really thinking about it.

"Would you like to come to a meeting with me sometime?" Zola said, almost nervously, Gina thought.

"I..." She didn't quite know what to say. She'd always thought that the meetings were something for adults, like open mouthed kissing or drinking the stinky cider. "Yes, please," she said, finally. She would still do anything for Zola.

There were only seven people in the room and Gina had seen most of them before in the neighbourhood. Reverend Sproule, of course, and Zola. Gina recognized Danny Fischmann, the medic's assistant, from the time she'd broken her ankle from jumping off the top of a train car. She smiled at him and saw his eyes go wide. He glanced at Zola who nodded and he smiled, but Gina could tell he was scared. Why would a big man like Mister Fischmann be scared of her, she thought. She was only eleven years old.

She sat next to Zola and waited. She was nervous, though she couldn't have explained why. It just felt like this was a big deal, a secret event that she'd been specially invited to. It seemed important and, even though she didn't know why, she felt proud to be allowed to be there.

Everyone had been chatting with each other, then all of a sudden they seemed to know to stop. They looked expectantly at Reverend Sproule, who was staring up at a spot in the ceiling. Gina looked up, too, but she didn't see anything particular there. She looked over at Zola, who was sitting quietly with her eyes closed. Nothing happened for what seemed like forever to Gina, so when Reverend Sproule finally spoke, Gina jumped.

"It is time," she said and the others responded, "time is everything." Then nothing happened for another long period. Gina's bottom was starting to get sore, but she could tell that she was supposed to be quiet and still. She wondered how long this was going to go on when one of the other people suddenly stood up. He was a young man, younger than Zola or her mother, and Gina had seen him before, but she couldn't remember where. He opened his eyes and began to talk.

"I can feel it," he said, "the passage of space around me." He paused and looked around the room. Gina wondered what that meant. "The illusion of change, the lie of death, it is all falling away as I focus my mind on the atoms around me. All praises to the master of all things, the mother of the universe."

"All glory to time, and to time all glory," the others intoned. Gina didn't understand any of it, but there was something magical about being with these people. The looks on their faces were serious yet full of some kind of joy she'd never seen before. They seemed to experience something very different in that room than Gina had ever seen. She wanted to feel what they felt.

After the service was over, Gina and Zola stayed behind. "What did you think?" Reverend Sproule asked Gina. She looked at Zola, wanting to say the right thing. She wanted to impress Reverend Sproule, to make her think she was smart and deserving. But she didn't know what to say.

"It's okay," Zola said, as if she could read Gina's fears in her face, "no one expects it to have made much sense to you."

Gina frowned. That sounded like the kind of thing that people said when they thought a kid couldn't understand something complicated, but Gina was good at figuring thing out. She understood a lot more than most grown-ups gave her credit for. Zola wasn't usually like that, though, so she let it pass. After all, the service really hadn't made much sense.

"Well," she started, "I didn't really understand what was going on. What that man talked about—I don't know what that meant. And at first it was kind of boring," she said, her face flushing with embarrassment, though Reverend Sproule smiled, so she went on. "But then, after a while, it was nice just sitting in the silence, letting everything kind of just go by. Like time sort of stopped for a bit, you know?"

Zola looked over at Reverend Sproule, her smile making Gina's heart beat faster. "I knew it," she said, her voice barely above a whisper.

Reverend Sproule nodded. "Gina, would you like to learn about something that is very important, in fact it is the most important information in the whole universe?" Gina nodded. "The thing is, it's secret knowledge. So secret, that just telling you about it could get me in a lot of trouble. These meetings, this worship we do, it's not allowed on the ship. So you need to know, before we go on, that there is a cost to this knowledge. Do you understand?"

Gina thought for a moment. She knew there were many things that weren't allowed on the ship—taking something that belonged to someone else, hurting other people, refusing to become a mother. But those things were all bad, she knew that, too. She couldn't imagine that Zola would ever do something bad, would let her do something that was bad. So this knowledge, these meetings, why would they be forbidden? She asked Reverend Sproule to explain.

The reverend sighed. "It's complicated," she said. "But most simply, it's because the people who make the rules don't believe that what we know to be true is true. And they don't like the consequences of what we know, either."

Gina frowned. "Consequences?"

"Yes," Zola said. "The way you believe the universe works affects the choices you make. It is the most important piece of understanding you have, because everything you do is based on that knowledge."

"So," Gina said, trying to put together everything they had said, "you believe the universe works differently from the way everyone else thinks it does. And people don't like that?"

"Exactly," Reverend Sproule said, smiling. "Now," she said, leaning forward in her chair and looking Gina squarely in the eye, "do you want to know?"

In the two years between Gina's first confused meeting and the day they had sentenced the others to confinement in the medical lab, Gina had spent all her free time studying the teachings. At first it was really just to please Zola and Reverend Sproule, but the more she learned the more she thought it just made sense. She had often wondered what came before the universe, what would happen when it finally crunched back in on itself. Because there had to be a before and there had to be an after, that was how everything worked.

But what if things didn't really work that way at all? What if, instead of time flowing through the universe, the universe flowed through time? What if time was the creator of matter, what if it was matter that was suffused with entropy but time stood still? Then there was no waiting, no need to hope. No fear of death. If all is now, then everything that was and all that will be exist now, too. The very possibility made Gina's eyes water.

She had known her whole life that she was part of the Glorious Middle—those who would never see a planet, never be held by real gravity. It wasn't something that had ever bothered her before, it was just reality. She hardly even thought about where people came from, where they were going, until she learned about Time.

When the medics came and took Zola away, Gina cried and cried. Her mother took two days off work to be with her, and spent the whole time apologizing for leaving Gina with a "religious freak." Gina knew she had to be careful, had to repudiate her closest friends, and it was so hard. The lies she told about them were half the reason for her tears, but her mother and the others believed them. Her mother said, more than once, that no daughter of hers would be poisoned by such ignorant thoughts.

"Worshipping *time*," she said, disgust clearly in her voice. "Who would think such a thing? A person might as well kneel before the great god of distance. How ridiculous. It's such a shame you had to listen to their nonsense, Gina my darling. I'm so sorry you had to go through this."

Gina nodded and sniffled and clenched her fists so hard the nails bit into the skin of her hands. "It's all right now, mother," she said. "I'm just glad that they'll finally get the help they need." As she said the acid words, in her mind, she prayed. Father of the past, mother of the future, hold my kin close to the heart of your spiral. Let them pass from this point in space to another, free from the indignities they suffer in your name's sake. Let it be, now as it is and as it was and evermore shall be.

It is one of the great things about ideas, about beliefs—they require only to live in your mind, they can be kept secret. Alone in her quarters, Gina worshipped daily. She developed a reputation as a bit of a loner, one of the quiet kids. Other members of her class at school were getting in trouble for wrecking the gardens with their parties and sneaking bottles of wine, but not Gina. Her teachers praised her studious nature and her mother was convinced that she would follow in her footsteps with a career in engineering. But when Gina left school, she chose to take the first job she could get. It was the closest she ever came to letting her secret out.

"But why?" her mother asked, "you would easily be accepted at the Academy if you applied."

"It's not for me," Gina had answered, knowing that this would be a battle.

"How do you know?" her mother had asked. "You would love the Academy, I'm sure of it. You always have your eyes on your tablet, I know you are smart enough. Why would you throw your future away like this?"

Gina had trained herself to never show her true feelings, or she would have laughed then. Throw away the future? How could that even be possible? The future is here, now, has always been here. There is no river, no arrow. Time cannot be constrained by a metaphor. Those forbidden thoughts filled her with resolve and she just shook her head. "This is what I want," she said with finality. "I'll be able to move into my own quarters once the probationary period is over, so I won't be here to embarrass you any more. If you can't wait, the placement officer said that I can find a room to share between now and then."

Her mother looked at Gina, a stunned expression on the older woman's face. Gina wondered if she had gone too far, if her mother would call the medics now in the face of her rebellion. But instead her mother turned away, a sob choking her, and retreated to her own bedroom. Gina realized then that her mother had completely forgotten about the nanny with her backward ideas, that it was just a minor inconvenience in her past. She realized that she had succeeded in fooling her mother completely, that she had truly believed that Gina was the studious, literate and unquestioning automaton she herself had been at that age.

In her room she sent a message to the placement officer at the water reclamation plant asking for temporary quarters and began to pack her things. For the first time in her life, she felt sorry for her mother, but it was too late.

After half a year, her mother had sent her a message asking if she was still happy in her job, along with the transfer of several thousand credits to "help get her on her feet." Gina knew it was just her mother's way of trying to reopen the door to convince her to abandon her own decision and returned the money with no return note.

Gina was happy then, content to do her menial work in exchange for being left alone to pursue her secret meditations. She wished she could start another group like the Reverend Sproule had begun, but she was still afraid of being caught. She had spent so long hiding her beliefs that didn't know how to talk to anyone about them. She was certain she would live and die alone and had come to almost cherish the idea. Then she met Devon.

He was in the most out of the way corner of the market. Gina had only stumbled across him and his small paintings by accident—a wrong turn after grocery shopping while her thoughts were elsewhere and then knocking into an easel. A frightened voice drew her out of her thoughts and she caught the painting before it fell to the ground. "I'm so sorry," she said, straightening the painting then stopping mid-thought as she took in its subject. It was a space scene, not uncommon among the ship's artists, but there was something about it that captivated her. Planets, satellites, comets, stars, nebulae—they were realistically depicted, but in a jumble, as if they were concentrated in space—or in time. She gasped. This man had painted a representation of the One Time. Could he possibly know?

"Whew," he said as she stepped back out of the thrall of the painting. "Thanks for catching that. It took me almost two years to finish."

"Wow," Gina said, "that's a lot of painting." She smiled and noticed that he smiled back at her. She rarely noticed other people, but he was lovely. His long, dark hair shone in the dim light of the market and his smile reminded her of Zola's. It made her sad and lonely, and she rarely acknowledged those feelings any more. "It's breathtaking," she said, jerking her head back in the direction of the painting, her breath quickening as he smiled again.

"Thank you," he said. "You're the first person who's actually made it all the way back here to see them," he admitted.

Gina remembered something Zola used to say—when it's right, time will tell. This is what she meant, Gina thought.

"It must just be the right time," she said.

"It was all a lie!" Kieran's mother shouted. At least it seemed like a shout to him; he realized later that she probably was trying to be quiet. Doubtlessly, she didn't want him asking inconvenient questions and she surely wouldn't want to have been heard by anyone else in the passageway outside their quarters. He'd probably only heard her because he'd opened the door to his room. He sat down next to the open door, as quietly as possible, and tried to hear the rest of the conversation.

"You can't know that, Lynn," his mother's friend Rachel said. "There's no reason to think that it's anything other that what we've been told. I mean, what would be the point of a lie?"

"Damn it, Rach," his mother said, and Kieran strained to hear her, "what would be the point? To keep us cooped up in here, agreeing to whatever they want us to do. Work in the refining plants, do our duty, get pregnant. Everything we do, it's because they tell us we have to. But how do we really know that any of it is real? They say we're on a ship, but I've never seen an engine, have you? They say we're going to a new planet, but how can we be sure? They say we have to live like this, but how can we know? No one knows what the crew quarters are like; they could be living like kings while we serve them like slaves."

"Lynn," Rachel said, her voice taking on the tone that Kieran always associated with the way teachers talk to the dumb kid in class. "Do you realize what you sound like? Paranoid. Crazy. You can't talk like this."

"I know," Kieran heard his mother say, and it sounded like her voice was muffled by something. He imagined her with her face in her hands—it was a pose she adopted often enough. "I just can't stop wondering..."

"Don't do anything... rash," Rachel said. "There has to be some way of knowing for sure."

Kieran frowned. Rachel was right; his mother did sound paranoid. Of course they were on a ship, he'd been to the observation room more times than he could count. It was obviously space out there. What did she think, that it was some elaborate hoax? For what purpose? Kieran shook his head. It was a good thing he was just about finished his welding apprenticeship. If she kept up like this, his mother would be landing in the medclinic for sure. And then he'd be on his own.

"You ever wonder what's going on up on the command deck?" Kieran asked Marta. She was about his mother's age but the similarities ended there. Marta had been a master welder for more years than Kieran had been alive and it showed. Her seams were nearly invisible, her hand as steady as a beam. Kieran didn't know if he wanted to be with her or to be her. Either way, he thought about her a great deal more than an apprentice should rightfully think about his master.

"Sure," Marta said, her eyes narrowing as she watched Kieran's work carefully. "I mean, everyone is curious. It's natural to wonder about the way things work, the meaning of it all. Why do you ask?"

"No reason," Kieran said, his hand trembling as he thought of his mother's tirade.

"Watch it, now," Marta said, her vigilant gaze catching his unsteadiness.

"Sorry," he said and tried to focus. He finished the weld and clicked the switch to shut off the safety field. He wiped his forehead and sat back, looking at his teacher.

"Not bad," Marta said, inspecting his work. "With several more years of practice, you'll be decent welder." Kieran tried not to smile —he knew this was as good a compliment as he could expect to receive from her. She picked up her tablet, poked and flipped pages, then paused and pressed her palm to the face of the machine. Kieran let the smile out now, knowing she'd just signed off on his apprenticeship.

"You're a good kid," she said, "but I can't do any more for you. You're on your own now, buddy. I've put your name on the active duty roster. In a few days you'll start getting job assignments." She looked at him squarely and Kieran almost thought he could see the corners of her mouth twitch. "Don't screw this up, boy. I don't want you making me look bad, got it?"

"Yes'm," Kieran said.

"All right," Marta said, then slapped him on his back. He momentarily couldn't breathe, she'd packed such a wallop. She began packing up the equipment and said, "Let's go get a beer."

They sat at a table in the middle of Scutter's, the Green Sector bar that catered to the trades. Kieran recognized a couple of other welding masters and a good half dozen of his fellow apprentices— correction, tradies. He hoisted his glass over to a knot of his peers and drank. He was on to his third pint and he hadn't eaten since lunch. It was a celebration, indeed.

"So, you've never been to the command deck?" he asked Marta, his drink sloshing on the already sticky tabletop.

"Hell no," she answered. "Far as I know, even the Chief hasn't been up there. Just gets messages through the usual channels."

Kieran thought about it. He knew Marta had met the Chief Engineer once, the legendary woman shook her hand. Almost crushed her with an iron grip, Marta'd said. "Don't they need welders?" he asked.

Marta shrugged. "Who knows? I mean, everything mechanical is down here—for all I know they don't really have anything but crew quarters and dance halls on C deck. Maybe they have their own welders, maybe machines do it? Who cares, anyway? The command crew might as well be, I dunno, a smart computer program for all we know. We get our orders, we do the jobs, we get paid, the ship keeps flying." She finished her drink and waved the empty toward the frazzled bartender. "Doesn't really matter what's going on up there, does it?"

"I guess not," Kieran said, but a small sober voice in the back of his mind told him that it probably mattered a great deal, indeed.

Kieran's new quarters were tiny, but they were all his. He could cross the whole space in a single long step but like the prince bound in a nutshell, he found himself king of infinite space. It was intoxicating.

When he was still living with his mother he had imagined scenarios that he realized now would never happen - parties, lovers, a young man's fantasy. Now he knew that even if he could find the people he would need to enact these visions he would have neither the time nor the energy. Tradie welders worked long hours.

But the freedom of being on his own was, as it turned out, enough excitement. The simplest things like visiting the market, preparing his simple meals, figuring out his finances—they were novel enough to keep him amused. For almost a half year, anyway.

He was visiting his mother for a meal. It was an event he'd first attended to regularly, but as time went on, her grasp of reality weakened and Kieran's ability to deal with her reduced. He was busy anyway, he told himself. She had given up trying to hide her concerns from him—maybe it was because now that he was on his own she perceived him as an equal, or maybe she just didn't care who knew what she thought. Regardless, her suspicions were almost all she ever talked about now.

"How do we know what's real and what isn't?" she ranted as

Kieran served the stew. He'd hoped that Rachel would join them, but she hadn't been over for one of their "family meals" in a while. He wondered if she had given up on his mother. "You look out the porthole and you're supposed to believe it's the universe out there. But no one really knows. We could be anywhere, trapped inside anything."

"Come on, mom," Kieran said, finally unable to keep quiet. "I've seen the fuel synthesizers myself, I worked on them just a few days ago. They're real, I promise."

She shook her head and Kieran knew that reasoning with her was pointless. He cursed himself for bothering, knowing it would lead to a bigger argument. "All you know is what they tell you," she said, waving her fork for emphasis. "If they told you those machines were cloud generators or waste recyclers, you'd believe that, too. You've no way of knowing, no way at all."

Kieran sighed and put his head down. He shovelled forkful after forkful into his mouth, hoping just to get to the end of the meal as quickly as possible. He loved his mother, he really did, but there was only so much more of this he could take.

The worst of it, of course, was that she was right. He really didn't know what most things he worked on did. And her incessant paranoia was starting to wear on him. What if this really wasn't a ship? What if something sinister really was going on? And how could he find out without becoming as crazy as his mother?

Kieran sat on his usual stool at the end of the bar in Scutters, nursing a glass of wine. He was lost in thought when he felt a hand heavy on his shoulder. He started, only barely managing to avoid spilling his drink, and turned to see the smiling face of his old teacher. "Marta," he said, slipping off his stool to slap her hand with his. "How've you been?"

"Never better," she said and hopped up to the seat next to

Kieran. She waved the bartender over and a pint of ale appeared quickly in front of her. "Heard you got a promotion at the shop this year. Good for you, buddy."

Kieran smiled. "Thanks. I'm finally starting to feel like I really know what I'm doing, you know?"

Marta nodded. "Yeah, takes a while before it all comes naturally." She took a drink then looked at Kieran thoughtfully. "For most of 'em, it never happens." Kieran felt her gaze on him, her exacting master's expectation making him feel like a green apprentice again. But he knew what she was saying and felt a flush of pride shoot through him. "Won't be too long before you get a greenie of your own. Then you'll know frustration, boy, let me tell you." She laughed and Kieran cocked his head.

"That's a long way off," he said. "I'm barely a Senior now."

"Time slips by without you looking. Trust me, it won't feel like too many days before your name's up on the board. I hardly remember my Senior days—it feels like it was something like two jobs and it was over." She signalled for another round, gesturing to Kieran's glass. He thought about it, then nodded. He'd forgotten how much he'd missed Marta's company.

"They are some jobs you remember, though," she went on as the bartender worked out their orders. "When you get up in the ranks you start to get to see parts of this ship you never even imagined." Their drinks arrived and she turned to face Kieran. He wondered if this bar weren't her first stop of the evening, but her eyes were sharp and her lips curled up into a grin. "Did you know that there's a whole room on November deck just for talking to dead people?"

Wine sputtered out of Kieran's nose and he grabbed for a nearby cloth. Marta laughed, her voice loud as Kieran began to sneeze. "What?" he finally managed to get out after coughing a few times.

"It's true," Marta said. "Back something like four generations they built this room with a bunch of little built-in tablets. It's like these private viewing booths, but not for regular stories. You use 'em to talk to personality constructs of people who were on board way back at the beginning of the voyage."

Kieran felt himself get completely sober in a hurry. "Are you serious?" he asked.

Marta nodded. "Yeah. No one knows about them anymore, I don't know why. Maybe it was a fad thing, or maybe they don't work right. They're probably just really boring. I mean, can you imagine someone five hundred years from now wanting to talk to a saved version of me about fixing a cold weld?" She rolled her eyes. "It's boring enough in real life." She took another drink and looked side-long at Kieran. "Still, it could be a funny way to spend an afternoon. I ought to go down there again sometime. See if I can find someone who can explain why they made those access tubes so damn narrow. Were they all just skinny little runts back then or what?"

Kieran barely heard her and had to focus on his breathing. He sipped his wine and nodded when it seemed appropriate to the con-versation, but his mind was gone. If only his mother had known, he kept thinking. It might have prevented her from...

"Hey, buddy, you okay?" Marta's voice broke through his reverie.

Kieran brought his focus back on his old teacher and saw a look of concern in her face. "Sure," he said. "I just... I guess I had one too many. I better get back to my quarters."

"Okay," Marta said. "You want I should make sure you get in okay?"

Kieran shook his head. "No," he said, "thanks anyway. I'll be fine." He slid off the stool and walked perfectly steadily to the door of Scutters.

"Hey, mom," Kieran said, trying to tamp down the guilty feeling which was rising in his chest. It had been a long time since he had last been to visit her. He had no excuse—he'd had enough time; with his new seniority had come not only a pay raise but more time off. No, he had just been avoiding her, there was no way to deny it.

She didn't seem to have noticed his absence, though. "Kieran, my boy." Her voice was thick with drugs. He wondered the last time he had been here if this really was an improvement. The doctors said it was, that his mother was no longer causing herself undue stress, but Kieran wasn't sure. What kind of a life was this, drugged into a stupor from which her real personality couldn't escape. It was as if she were in a black hole of enforced sanity. Kieran actually missed his ranting, raving, paranoid mother.

"Rachel came to see me a few days ago," she went on, her voice slow and methodical. "She seemed so sad, but she wouldn't tell me anything."

Kieran shook his head, swallowing hard to keep himself in check. "I'm sure Rachel is fine, mom," he said, finally. "You just worry about getting better."

His mother frowned. "I wish I knew what was wrong with me," she said. "The doctors tell me they can't explain it to me, but it's hard to know if I'm getting any better if I don't know what's wrong."

"I know, mom," Kieran said, the tightness in his chest threatening to cut off his breathing. As it was, he was beginning to feel lightheaded. "I'd better go," he said, reaching over to hold his mother's hand. "I don't want to tire you out."

"No," his mother said, agreeing, but she sounded unsure. She always sounded unsure, now.

"I love you, mom," Kieran said, his voice cracking. He cleared his throat. "I— I'm going to see if we can get you out of here."

"That would be nice, sweetie," she said, her heavy-lidded eyes closing. "I think I'd like that..." She seemed to be drifting back into some half-asleep fugue, and Kieran used the opportunity to escape.

It took him longer than it ought to have before he finally called Marta. He had never contacted her socially and it felt strange, like he was doing something naughty or transgressive. He liked the feeling.

"Good to hear from you," Marta said, and Kieran wondered if she was this friendly with all her apprentices. "What's new in the world of pipes?"

"You don't know?"

"Not really," Marta said and Kieran saw her face take on a cloudy look. "They've got me on admin duty these days." She lifted a hand up to the camera and Kieran could see her once steady-as-a-rock fingers trembling. She dropped her hand and shrugged. "The price of getting older," she said. "Beats the alternative. So, to what do I owe the pleasure?"

At first Kieran didn't know what to say. All he could think of were her quivering hands. He couldn't imagine what he would do if he couldn't weld—and he was nowhere near the artisan Marta was. He had to force himself back to the moment.

"Remember when I saw you in Scutters last? Must have been, what—a half year, something like that?" Marta nodded. "Well, you were talking about those weird rooms on November deck? With the dead people?"

"Sure," Marta said. "What about them?"

Kieran paused. What did he want? What did he think he could learn from a bunch of simulated people? "Did you ever try it out?" he asked finally. "Did you talk to any of them?"

He saw Marta smile. "Yeah," she said. "They told me not to fool with any of the doodads in there, but how could I not? I mean, wouldn't you want to talk to someone from the past if you could?"

"Yes," Kieran said, nodding solemnly. He hadn't even realized it himself, not consciously. "Yes, I would very much like to talk to one of them."

Marta grinned. "Well, then, my boy. It looks like we have a bit of a secret mission to embark on, eh?"

They met outside the door to the lift on November deck. Kieran was shocked at how old Marta looked—the comms had blurred the wrinkles around her eyes and she somehow seemed smaller than he remembered her. When she clapped a hand on his shoulder, though, he could still feel the strength in her grip. "I checked the master job board," she said, her voice low. "There's no work scheduled down here for a few days and there's no reason for anyone to be in this section at all." She grinned at him. "It's supposed to be off-limits."

Kieran felt his heart beating and wondered for the first time how much trouble they could get in if they were caught. As if she could read his thoughts, Marta said, "I don't think anyone really cares. Besides, no one is supposed to be down here, so who's going to know? C'mon, let's go." She took off down the corridor and Kieran had to hurry to keep up. Maybe she wasn't so feeble after all.

It looked more like the door to an access hatch than the entrance to an electronic mausoleum. "You sure this is it?" he asked.

"Definitely," Marta said and looked up and down the corridor as if expecting some authority to catch them in the act. She grinned again and Kieran wondered how long it had been since she'd done anything fun. He also wondered why anyone would find this fun— he was having fifth thoughts by now. Marta opened up the access panel and punched in a maintenance override code. A shockingly loud *beep* sounded then the door popped open.

"All right," she said and shouldered open the door. "Let's go have a chat."

The room was as Marta had described—like a cinema, but with a dozen small screens. It had a funny smell that Kieran associated with barely-used access ducts. "How long has it been since anyone was in here?" he asked and Marta shrugged.

"Far as I know, I'm the only one who's been in here for years," she said. "C'mon, pick one." She grinned and elbowed Kieran in the ribs. He looked around but the stations all looked the same.

"Are they different people?" he asked.

"I dunno," Marta said. "I only tried one and it gave me a list to pick from. Beats me why they needed so many screens." She walked around the room slowly, eyeing the devices. "Maybe when they built this it was so popular they needed to serve a bunch of people at once. Who knows why they built anything the way they did around here." She shook her head and Kieran smiled at her familiar complaint. "Let's try this one," she said, slipping into the seat in front of the screen furthest from the door. Kieran walked up behind her and watched as she powered on the device.

"They'll know we turned it on," he said and Marta laughed.

"Sure," she said, "if anyone's monitoring this place, which I doubt. I don't even think anyone remembers it's here." She poked at the screen and Kieran saw a list of names and faces appear. "Besides, I already did this once and nothing happened. We'll be fine." She turned to Kieran and the wrinkles around her eyes deepened as she grinned at him. "Squeeze in here and let's take a walk down memory lane."

Kieran felt an almost electrical surge through his body as he sat next to Marta, their thighs touching on the narrow bench. He kept his eyes focussed on the dim screen. There were a long list of names and faces, all women, all looking older than Marta was now. Kieran shrugged. "I dunno," he said. "How about her?" He pointed at a woman called Audra Tamehana. She had kind eyes.

Marta poked at the screen and it went blank. For a moment, Kieran wondered if they'd broken something, then the woman's face filled the screen. She blinked twice, then seemed to look first at Marta then at Kieran. "Well, hello," she said, the voice coming from a speaker on the side of the screen. "How nice to have visitors."

"I do not wish to seem rude," Audra said, after they'd awkwardly introduced themselves, "but you appear to be a young man."

Kieran blushed, though he didn't really understand why. "I am twenty-four," he said. "Is that... a problem?"

Audra and Marta laughed, and seemed to share some kind of look between them that Kieran didn't understand. "Not at all, my dear," Audra said. "Though it wasn't your age which surprised me."

Kieran frowned and looked at Marta. She just angled her head back to the screen as if he should ask Audra. As he turned back to the screen Audra said, "In my time there were very few boys. And no young men at all. It is, in fact, quite wonderful to see that things have obviously changed. I'm guessing it must have been some time since I last had a visitor. Tell me, what generation are you?"

"We don't count that way anymore," Marta said to Kieran's utter confusion. "But we're a bit more than halfway to new Earth. There was a big celebration to mark it when I was young."

"Ah," Audra said, a wide smile lighting her face. "How wonderful." She appeared to look at the two of them, and Kieran felt uncomfortable being scrutinized by a machine. "Well, I doubt you fired me up just to give me an update on our journey. Tell me, what is it you'd like to know? Why did you wake me?"

Marta turned to Kieran when he didn't say anything and asked, "Well, kid? Why are we here?"

"I guess I just want to know what it was like," Kieran said, finally, after humming and hawing and making Audra and Marta laugh. "Back at the beginning. When the ship set out." He watched Audra's face carefully, looking for some indication that she knew that it was all a ruse. But her face held the same expression of equal parts amusement and edification.

"I was part of generation eight," she said. "That's the eighth group of children to be born after the ship launched. By the time I was born, none of the initial crew were alive, but my great-great-grandmother would tell me stories that she'd heard from her great-great-gran. How there were whole decks of the ship that were closed off, because there were so few people. It was a time of great change, of experimentation, even when I was a girl. No one had really known what would happen after years and years on a ship alone in space. How we would live, how we would make a community here."

She closed her eyes as if remembering those moments so long ago. "Sometimes I felt like I was a slave to the knowledge of our greatness, a greatness which had more to do with an accident of birth than anything innate within ourselves. We were just the ones who came after, just the ones entrusted to keep our mission alive. The ones who were truly great, who left old Earth behind to find a new home for us all, they were gone. And yet every day I knew that I was a part of something amazing, a journey into the future that would dwarf every other human endeavour."

She opened her eyes again and Kieran felt an intensity in her gaze that crossed the gulf of centuries, the reality of her long-ago death. "It is a heroic life you lead, young man," she said and Kieran felt the words crash into him. "All of us who have been privileged to live on this ship. If you learn anything from history, learn that."

Kieran nodded dumbly, his voice lost. Marta thanked Audra and shut down the machine. "You find what you were looking for?" she asked as they left the room. Kieran nodded again, still unable to speak. He wondered if he could find a way to bring his mother here, to let her listen to this voice from the past.

Kieran knew there was nothing the personality construct had said that even came close to proof that the stories were true. Nothing that couldn't just be part of a grand lie to keep people like him, like Marta, like Rachel and his mother quiet and compliant. But he knew that if his mother could hear Audra's story that everything would change. Because Audra would make her want to believe. As Kieran did.

Beatriz walked down the darkened corridor, one hand along the bulkhead as a guide. She cursed under her breath. This was the fifth outage is as many days – clearly someone had lost the plot down in power management. But of course she was the one who was woken and asked to crawl around in the dark to fit a new fuse. Typical. It was going to be a long night.

There was one advantage to this recurring problem, though. She knew her way to the Green Sector power relay in her sleep. She strode purposefully down the hall, knowing that she'd reach the access panel in a few seconds. She felt the outline of the hatch and stopped, finding the release catch and popping open the recessed door. She carefully set the cover next to the now-exposed hatch and peered into the opening. She couldn't see a thing.

She knelt down and crawled into the service tube. This was the worst part. She could feel the walls of the small space closing in on her, even though she knew they were solid. She fought with herself not to turn on her headlamp, knowing there was only enough power in the cell to keep the light ablaze for fifteen minutes. She also knew that it could take that much time to switch out the fuse, so she had to conserve.

Not for the first time, she cursed the poor planning that left her with such an underpowered light. "You can tap into the ship's power from anywhere," they said. "There's no need for portable lights," they said. She let her annoyance smother her fear as she crawled as quickly as she could to the fuse box.

She palmed open the box and felt around in her pocket for the new fuse. Only when it was in her hand did she finally switch on her headlamp. She squinted at the sudden brightness, then began the task of determining which fuse had blown and replacing it.

When she was done, a low hum filled the space and the lights blinked back on. She took a breath and began backing out of the tube. She felt something brush her leg and she let out an involuntary squeal. She rolled on to her back and sat up, her heart racing. She saw a flash of movement and turned toward it, her hands clenched into fists. She was just about to lash out when she recognized the source of the movement.

"Thomas?" she asked, her face screwed into a frown. "What are you doing here?"

The young boy shrugged and Beatriz shook her head. Thomas was her sister's boy, and he had always been a bit odd. Quiet, not the rough and tumble handful her other nieces and nephews were. At first, Beatriz had found the boy's calmer nature to be a relief, but as he'd grown older it had become a little off-putting. And now he was following her around.

Great.

"Does your mother know where you are?" Beatriz asked as they scooted toward the glow of the hatch's opening into the corridor.

"How can I know what she knows?" Thomas asked, methodically moving along the ground in front of Beatriz. It was as if he'd been here before. She felt a shiver go up her spine. Kids. They were creepy at the best of times. These were not the best of times.

"We should probably be getting you home," she said. "Your mom will be worried." Thomas didn't answer, and Beatriz wondered if he could tell that she was trying to get rid of him. She wanted to go back to her quarters, pour a drink and relax. She hadn't had a decent sleep since the first outage and it was starting to take its toll. She hoped she'd be able to keep her temper with Thomas.

They reached the hatch and Thomas scooted into the corridor. He made no move to leave, just stood across the hall waiting for

Beatriz. She pulled herself out of the hatch, grunting with effort, and stood. She patted her pockets to check that she'd remembered all her tools, then lifted the hatch cover back into position. It clicked into place and locked with a hiss of compressed air. Beatriz turned to her nephew and a chill passed through her body. He was staring at her with an intensity that she did not enjoy.

"Come on, buddy," she said, turning down the corridor. "Let's get you home."

They walked toward the habitation sector, alone in the corridor. It was late and few people had cause to be in this part of the ship. Beatriz often marvelled at how much empty space there was on the enormous starship. A few generations down the line some of these areas would become habitation sectors, but now there were whole sections that were almost as empty as the vacuum on the other side of the hull.

They turned a corner and Beatriz realized that Thomas had been staring at her the entire time. She didn't know what to say to a six-year-old, but the silence was worse than an inane conversation.

"You're pretty quiet. There must be a lot going on up there," she said, tapping her own temple.

Thomas made no response. It was as if he hadn't heard her at all. She stopped walking, and he stopped as well, his attention never leaving her face. She knelt in front of him. His wide-open blue eyes never wavered from her gaze. "You okay, buddy?" she asked. "Staring at me is kind of weird, you know?"

"I just want to see if there's anything there," he said.

"Okay," Beatriz said, forcing a laugh. "You know what they say? 'The eyes are the windows to the soul.' That it?"

Thomas frowned. "What's windows?"

Beatriz laughed, legitimately this time. She stood and waved Thomas over to the side of the corridor. "Like the ports in the observation deck. They let you see what's on the other side. Like this."

At the wall-mounted terminal, she hit a few keystrokes. A live feed from one of the exterior cameras filled the screen. She lifted Thomas up so he was facing the image.

He scrutinized the picture for a moment, then repeated, "Windows to the soul." He wriggled around in Beatriz's arms and stared at her again. His eyes were so clear, so blue, like the images of Earth's sky she'd seen once. He looked at her intently for what felt like forever. Finally, he blinked once and said, "There's nothing there."

Beatriz put him down. He was no longer looking at her, but rather up at the screen, its display still showing the darkness of space. "There's nothing there," he repeated, then walked down the corridor toward his quarters.

Beatriz didn't follow him and he didn't look back at her. Why would he?

Back in her quarters, Beatriz poured a large drink. She sat, sipping, thinking about Thomas. He was just a child. He didn't know anything, was probably just going through some phase. She didn't envy her sister, that was certain. But she couldn't stop thinking about what he'd said.

What if he were right? What if there was nothing there, nothing for them to aim for, no planet for them to one day call home? What if they were out in the void, literally going nowhere?

And, worse, what if there was nothing inside either? Nothing special about humanity that made them worth saving?

Beatriz downed her drink and poured another. It was going to be a long night, indeed.

The birds hid in the trees. They had no predators, no need to fear anyone or anything, but their ancient instincts still told them to conceal themselves among the leaves, their presence only indicated by their tentative calls to one another. Neils walked quietly among the branches, careful not to snap a twig or rustle the leaves. According to his supervisor, within a few generations the birds would learn to be unafraid. It was a shame.

Neils stopped at the foot of a healthy rimu and stood very still. There were a half dozen birds on its branches and he knew that if he moved too suddenly they would fly off. He'd done this hundreds of times before, but catching birds was one of the harder parts of his job. It was also among the most fun.

After waiting several minutes, he sprung his trap. He managed to get three birds in the wire cage, the area filled with the sound of their terrified flapping and squawking. "Shhh," he said softly, "quiet, now. I'm not going to hurt you." The birds continued their caterwauling and, although the sound was piercing, Neils smiled. It was good that they had a sense of self-preservation, good that they maintained some independence from the human population which ensured their continued survival. He picked up the cage and carried it out of the woods.

"A healthy bunch," Celine said, peering into the cage. "Any trouble catching them?"

"Naw," Neils said. "They aren't getting any smarter."

Celine looked up at him sharply. "You can't apply our standards of intelligence to another species," she said. "That's the kind of anthropocentric thinking that made old Earth the mess it was."

Neils shrugged. He couldn't have given a definition of the word "anthropocentric," but he knew what his boss meant. She was always talking like that, but she went to the Academy. She was a zoologist; Neils was just a wildlife assistant. He liked animals and knew that he was lucky to get to work with them. There weren't that many out of cryo—a dozen species of birds, some insects, the rodents and the fish. He didn't deal with the fish or the bugs, though. Those were different specialities. He was happy enough with his birds and mammals. They never used words he didn't understand in order to make themselves feel superior.

"I'm just saying I didn't notice any behavioural changes, that's all," Neils said, meeting Celine's eyes. He saw the dark skin of her face redden slightly and managed to keep the smile off his face. "You want a hand getting them out?"

Celine nodded. "Yes, thanks. Can you grab the gloves?" He got two pairs of long, heavy gloves and handed a pair to Celine. They both put on the protective gear, then Neils opened two small hatches on the cage. He carefully slipped his hands inside and held on to the birds. "Ready?" she asked.

"Yeah," he said. "Go for it." Celine opened the main door of the cage and thrust her hand inside. She held a bulky syringe unit and while Neils held the birds she injected them with a mild tranquilizer. Soon they all fell limp and Neils extracted his hands. "Easy as," he said, smiling. "Anything else?"

"No, I've got it from here," she said. "I'll get the data I need, give them a little check up, and they'll be ready for reintroduction in, say, four hours?"

"I'll be back before I knock off for the day, then," he said. "Give me a shout if you need anything."

"I will," she said, then turned back to the bird, lying almost lifeless on the counter.

Neils left the aviary and entered the main corridor of Blue Sector. There were a lot of people coming and going at this time in the day and he recognized few of them. He didn't really spend a lot of time with that many people—Celine, of course, Jan, the other assistant, and his buddy Kiew. Other people didn't really interest him. He preferred his animals. He kept his head down and walked directly to the mammal lab. It was down a level on Lima deck, so he had to walk a good fifteen minutes, but he didn't mind. There wasn't anything special going on today, just the regular maintenance.

He got to the lab and ran through the usual procedure—food, water, checking for any problems. The animals in here were all still caged. Neils didn't know when, or if they would be released into a more natural environment. His job didn't require him to know. He hoped they would, even if it meant he wouldn't get to interact with them as much. It seemed wrong to keep an animal in a cage.

After he was done with the gerbils, hamsters, ferrets and the rest, he figured he had an hour or two before he'd need to be back at the aviary. And he needed feeding and watering as much as the animals did, so he set off for his quarters. He preferred to eat there rather than at a canteen, always full of other people. In ten minutes he was in his small quarters, staring at his food storage area, trying to figure out what to eat.

His handheld buzzed and he sighed. Probably Celine needing help. He picked it up and saw that it was Kiew instead. He smiled. "Hi," he said, "I was just about to have lunch. Want to come over?"

"Okay," Kiew's voice came out of the small speaker. "See you in a few."

He'd only gotten a salad made when the door to his quarters chirped. "Come in," he said and the door swished open at his voice command. Kiew walked into the galley and sat on zir usual chair.

"How hungry are you?"

"Just salad's good," zie said. "How did the bird capture go?"

"Same as always," he said, placing a bowl in front of Kiew. He handed zir a fork and zie started to eat. "Celine almost went off on one of her 'old Earth' rants again, though."

Kiew rolled zir eyes. "Who do they think they're fooling?" zie asked between bites.

"I don't know," Neils said. "Sometime I think she really believes it, the way she gets so passionate about our so-called origins. But, come on. She's educated and she's not dumb. But why pretend?"

"They want to keep the rest of us in our place, that's why." Kiew had some radical political views. Neils didn't exactly share them, but he didn't think zie was entirely wrong, either.

"And you really think that by pretending we have some far-fetched history accomplishes that?" He bit into a piece of bread, and sat back to enjoy Kiew's upcoming tirade.

"It's not just the history and you know it," zie said. "It's the whole narrative. *We're on a heroic journey, the last survivors of a dying race, the saviours of humanity.* I mean, you've got to admit, it's a lot easier to get people to do what you want to them to do with the weight of that kind of story behind it."

"But why bother with any of it?" Neils countered. "Why bother with this complicated reason for our situation? I mean, it's obvious we're stuck on a ship."

"Is it?" Kiew asked. Neils sighed.

"You can see the stars outside, Kiew."

"No," zie said, "you can see something on a screen that they say are the stars outside. I've never seen a porthole, have you?"

"No," Neils said, "but it fits the rest of the evidence that I have seen." He started ticking points off on his fingers. "A finite space, fabricated out of plastic and metal. Reduced gravity on the upper deck levels including the weightless room. A huge aeronautical engineering program. Careful botanical and zoological management for a closed system."

Kiew shook zir head as he enumerated his arguments. "Points one and four could relate to any closed environment. And point three could be more of their lies to throw us off."

"What about the gravity?"

Kiew looked at him askance. "Are you a physicist now?" zie asked.

"No," Neils said. "But I know how to use spin to create force." He picked up a towel and started spinning it over his head. He let go and it flew straight into Kiew's face. Zie started to laugh, then threw it back at him.

"Fair enough," zie said. "I didn't really think that idea was going to fly. But still, a ship isn't a prison. Just because we're stuck here doesn't mean we have to live like slaves. People like you and me can never be anything more than the staff—we're just here to make everything work for the ones who matter, up on the top decks."

Neils shrugged. "I don't know about *slavery*, Kiew," he said. "Besides, none of us will see new Earth no matter what deck we're on, no matter what school we went to. So, really, who cares? Anyway, I *like* my work, when I don't have to deal with people."

"Well, that's because you don't work in waste reclamation."

He laughed. "It's suits you, you're so full of shit." His handheld chirped then, and he picked the towel off his shoulder. "I have to go back to the birds," he said. "You coming over after?"

"I can't," Kiew said. "I'm on second shift for the next while."

"Okay," Neils said. "Well, I'd better get going."

"I'll clean this up," Kiew said, "see you later."

When Neils arrived at the aviary, he was a little early. "I've still got one bird to examine," Celine said when he walked in the door. "You can come back if you want."

"It's okay," Neils said. "I've got a few things to do around here." He began tidying up the lab, his mind on his conversation with Kiew. Zie just enjoyed arguing, usually the more far-fetched the better. Though zie was right about one thing—there wasn't any conclusive proof about a lot of the things they'd been told about their journey. And so much of what came out of the leadership and the Academy was so obviously mythological garbage, that it did make him wonder what you could believe.

He looked over at Celine, who was carefully handling a now-awake but groggy starling. He'd had his differences with her over the years, certainly, but there was no doubt that she cared about the animals as much as he did. Of course, her idea of concern was to capture them, inject them with drugs and make sure they developed properly. Neils was no biologist, but he thought the birds would be happier left alone, hidden in the trees.

"All done," Celine said, as the last bird began to feebly flutter its wings. She put it back into the wire cage with its fellows and took off her gloves. "They're doing great," she said. "I'll have to analyze the samples I took to know more, but all in all I'd say that we can all be really proud of the avian project." She stepped back and smiled broadly at Neils. "This is a great contribution to the mission. It feels good to be making history, don't you think."

"Sure," Neils said, picking up the cage. "I'm going to get these guys back where they belong now."

"All right." Celine's smile faded. "Thanks for your help." Neils nodded and left.

He opened the first door to the forest as the birds regained their voices. They obviously didn't like the tranquilizers, and were always loud once the drugs wore off. He waited for the outer door to close, then opened the inner door. Once it had closed, he gave it a little tug to be sure before opening the cage. He was careful to keep away from the hatch as the birds fought to escape. They flew off into the trees and it took only seconds before Neils couldn't see them anymore. He could still hear them, though.

He went through the careful double door procedure to make sure none of the forest creatures got out, then walked back to the lab with the empty cage. He thought about the birds.

They didn't need stories about how they were the most heroic starlings ever, living carriers of precious DNA across the years of space and time. They didn't need to believe that they came from a forest of unimaginable beauty and fragility, that they had allowed it to be destroyed, and their penance was to be trapped in a cage for generations until they finally reached a new tree full of possibility and promise.

The birds didn't need any of that—they still sang.

"Such is the force of magic and my spells."

A pop, a groan and the room filled with gasps of awe. Elly couldn't keep the smile from her face, but it was dark and everyone was transfixed by Mephistophilis and his materialization out of thin air.

"Now Faustus, what wouldst thou have me do?"

"That was brilliant, El!" Gryff's makeup was smudged and there were streaks where he'd been sweating, but he didn't seem to mind. "You are a genius."

Elly shrugged but she was proud of this set design. It was the first she'd done on her own and was more complicated than any of the others she'd helped with. "I'm just glad it worked," she said. "I had nightmares about you being trapped halfway out of the floor, looking up at Faust like a little kid."

"I'm a baby devil!" Gryff squealed in falsetto and laughed. "I never had a doubt. You're a genius," he repeated.

One of the other actors appeared—not in a puff of smoke from a clever device in the floor but from around a corner—and Gryff's attention was pulled away. Elly didn't mind. Gryff was a good actor and had developed a following after the last production. People were saying that he might be able to start a full-time theatre. Everyone wanted a moment of his time.

Elly left the two and slipped out the backstage door into the corridor. It was late and the silence of the passageway echoed after the boisterous theatre. "How did I ever end up doing this?" Elly wondered as she began the long walk back to her quarters.

She was on her third trip to the canteen for a cup of tea when Taha caught up with her. "Up late last night?"

Elly sighed. It was almost certainly a perfectly innocent question, but she couldn't help but read into it. For what felt like the millionth time, she chided herself for getting invoked with a colleague, even if they had managed to avoid the drama most workplace romances developed when they failed.

"Yeah," she said, fighting to take the question at face value. "It was the opening."

Taha's face creased in confusion and Elly felt a wave of heat that was part annoyance, part tiredness and partly an uncomfortable reminder of why she'd gone against her better judgment in the first place. "The opening?"

"Yeah, the play." She blew on her tea then took a sip. It was too hot but she drank it anyway.

"I forgot you were involved in that," Taha said, nearly brushing against her while reaching for a mug. "How'd it go?"

"Really good," Elly said. She wanted to talk about how she'd solved the problem of having performers appear and disappear all over the stage, of the prototypes she'd made, how she'd tinkered and fiddled until it was just right. She wanted to share that with someone who would understand—Gryff and the other theatre people knew it was difficult and were suitably impressed but they weren't interested in the technical details. Taha would be. But...

"Yeah, it was fine," she said and turned. "See you." She walked out of the canteen and back to her workshop, feeling petty, relieved and a little bit sad.

"Mom!" André launched himself at Elly as she walked through the door of their quarters. She scooped him up and they enjoyed a cuddle as she settled on the sofa.

"What exciting things did you get up to today, sweetie?"

"We practiced letters and numbers and tomorrow we're going to the weightless room in the centre of the ship!"

"Wow," Elly said, "I wish I was going to the weightless room tomorrow."

"So come with us." André looked at her with earnest seriousness.

"I can't sweetie. Mommy has to go to work."

"Why?"

Elly couldn't suppress the smile. She knew some parents found the relentless questions of their children maddening, but she loved André's irrepressible curiosity. And it was a perfectly legitimate question.

"Well, someone has to build the things we all use and that's what I do. If I didn't go to work, then someone's quarters wouldn't have a table or a galley or something else they need. And I like building things. It's fun."

"More fun than going to the weightless room with me?"

"Aw, sweetie, you know I love being with you more than anything. But you know how you can't just do whatever you want at school—you can't play all day, sometimes you have to learn letters or numbers. Well, it's the same for me. That's why Sandy stays with you after school." Elly looked up and caught the eye of the babysitter. Sandy was one of Elly's neighbour's kids and had a been a lifesaver. The teenager shot her a sympathetic glance.

"Okay," André said and snuggled into Elly's embrace. The topic was obviously settled to his satisfaction.

"See you tomorrow," Sandy said and Elly nodded.

"Come on," Elly said, "let's do something fun before supper."

André was sleeping soundly, so Elly settled into the couch with her tablet. The Faustus set was working fine, but she felt like there was room for improvement to her system. It relied on strong stagehands and perfect timing—there had to be a way to simplify it. She rotated the three-dimensional model, absent-mindedly worrying her bottom lip. She had that maddening feeling like the answer was right in front of her but she just couldn't see it. It wasn't helping that she was still thinking about running into Taha that afternoon.

They weren't well suited to one another. Her mother had said as much when it ended and Elly had agreed. Though how much of it was just coming up with an explanation to try and make Elly feel better, she sometimes wondered. But it seemed that they truly did have profoundly different world views. Elly remembered endless good-natured but unresolved disagreements about so many things: Elly's love of family life, her interest in theatre; frankly, her interest in anything other than the relationship. She always felt Taha was singular-minded, interested in a simple life of work and partnership, with everything else a distant second, if even considered.

It wasn't as though Taha had discouraged Elly's other interests—she'd never have been with someone who had. Instead it was as if Elly's eclecticism were some alien artifact—fascinating but baffling. She remembered one night when they'd gone to a concert. She'd asked Sandy to watch André, who was still too young to sit through a whole symphony. At the intermission, she'd turned to Taha and said, "I can't wait until I can bring André to something like this. He'd adore those trumpets and trombones, I can tell."

Taha squeezed her hand. "You don't have to worry about him, you know. Sandy is very responsible for a teen and he'll be fine."

Elly had frowned. "I'm not worried."

"Then why bring him up? Aren't you enjoying yourself?"

"Of course, I'm enjoying myself. That's why I thought of him—because he would enjoy it, too, and I can't wait to share it with him."

The lighting dimmed then and the cacophony of the orchestra's tuning ended their conversation. As the swell of music began, Elly wondered whether Taha even perceived of children as other people with interests and tastes, that she could feel more than just the love that comes with responsibility toward her son. That she could genuinely like him as another person.

The memory came with a wave of sadness. Elly wasn't sure how much of the feeling was for the lost relationship and how much for what she was now starting to recognize as pity for Taha's viewpoints. She picked up her tablet again and refocussed on the Faust set. There just had to be a way to make the system easier.

"Sorry I'm late."

Taha's voice was muffled by the cabinet in which Elly was crammed, but she recognized it easily. Wu was supposed to be on this job with her; what was Taha doing here? She carefully backed out of the cabinet, conscious of the fact that her rear end would be prominently displayed until she could extricate herself from the small space.

"Where's Wu?"

"Morning sickness."

"I didn't know she was pregnant." Elly could practically hear Taha shrug. Babies, family, other people's lives—they were trivia that Taha found tedious. Elly popped out of the cabinet and stood, stretching out her back. "I'm just about done with the interior finishing. Want to start on the countertops?"

"Why don't I finish up in there?" Taha said. "You look like you've been cramped up in a tiny space for too long."

Damn. Faults notwithstanding, Taha could be a sweetheart. "Sure. I'm going to grab tea then I'll be back." She tried not to hurry to the door of the half-finished quarters. She forced herself to stop and turned back. "Thanks."

Taha nodded, then started gingerly climbing into the cabinet.

There was no one in the canteen but Elly took her time with the tea. She wished she could move on, treat Taha like any other colleague. There was never any indication of ill will between them, and Taha had never pressured her into rekindling their romance. Elly knew it was all her, all her own conflicted feelings. She had been the one to end it and it had been the right decision. But she couldn't help that she still cared for Taha; some part of her still longed for them to be together.

She couldn't stay in the canteen forever, so walked back to the quarters they were working on. The muffled sounds of construction emanated from the cabinet, and she picked up her tablet to consult the plans for the counters. She picked up her tools, so perfectly moulded to her hands, and began to work. As usual for her, it didn't take long before that sense of flow took over and the counters seemed to assemble themselves under her hands. It was only the absence of sound from the cabinet that brought her out of focus to realize that Taha was standing behind her.

"Shift's over."

"Yeah, I guess," Elly said, wiping her forehead with a dusty hand. "Ought to be done in here tomorrow."

Taha nodded. "Wu will probably be back. I'm just filling in for people right now."

"Oh yeah," Elly said looking at Taha. "That's too bad. It was nice working together."

Taha's gaze held her for a long time and Elly wondered what her former partner was feeling. She'd never really known. Taha was a puzzle in so many ways—that was a big part of what she'd been drawn towards. Did Taha miss her, too? Was Elly the only one who knew that they were no good for each other, but secretly missed the tension?

"See you around," Taha said with a small smile, then turned and walked out of the room. Elly let a laugh escape. She would never know, would she?

"Shh," Sandy said as Elly walked into her quarters. "He's out like a light."

"I'm not surprised," Elly said. "I remember my first time in the weightless room. I think I pulled every muscle in my body." She walked into the galley and fished around in the tea drawer. Something calming. She needed to get a decent sleep tonight. Maybe she should go bouncing around with André. She looked up and was surprised to see Sandy still there.

"Everything okay?" she asked.

"Sure. Just, uh, I dunno..." Sandy avoided her eyes and Elly hoped that her neighbour wasn't going to quit the babysitting job. She didn't want to make anyone do anything they weren't enjoying, but Sandy was a great babysitter.

"It's okay," she said. "You can talk to me."

Sandy glanced over at Elly then looked away again. "I just—how do you do it? You seem so keen on everything. Your work, André, the theatre stuff. It's like even if you could do anything, even if you weren't trapped here, you'd still choose the life you have."

"My life isn't perfect, Sandy." She thought about Taha, about what it was like to love someone so utterly wrong for you, yet so strongly that you couldn't even think of looking elsewhere. "Not by a long shot." The teen's face took on that look that Elly remembered from her own youth—that an adult was being patronizing. "But you're not wrong, I am happy. I do like my job; I love André and the theatre work. Maybe I'm just lucky that I have an aptitude for things that are useful. Or maybe there are more opportunities than it seems. I know a lot of people spend their lives wishing for things to be different in a way they never can be. But there are so many things that make life meaningful here, it seems to me it's only a matter of finding what works for you."

She took a sip of tea and looked around her quarters. André's toys were scattered over the space, mixed among her tablets and schematics. "I know that doesn't sound very helpful, but it's true. Work and family are like doors. They can lock you in, or they can open up and let you out."

"Good morning class. All right, all right, settle down, now. Juli, stop that! Okay, now can I get you all to turn on your desks and jump to the history bookmark? Everyone there? Good.

"So yesterday we talked about the selection process for the ship's company, and now we're going to focus on one part of that group in particular. Can anyone tell me who the most important people were in the beginning of the voyage? Yes, Kristina?"

"Was it the nutritionists?"

"No, though that's a good guess."

"But everyone needs to eat."

"That's true, Sam, but they brought pre-made food with them for the first part of the trip. The nutritionists, botanists, farmers and chefs would become important soon, but not immediately. And, Sam, next time don't forget to ring in before you speak, okay? Good.

"No, try to think about who would be absolutely crucial right from the start. People who would be doing things that the entire mission would depend on.

"...

"Anyone?

"...

"Yes, Becky, you look like you might have an idea."

"Um... what about the bridge crew?"

"Exactly! The people who fly the ship, who navigate the stars! In those first few days of the voyage, they were the only people standing between success and failure for the First Heroes of the *White Cloud*. So let's hear a little bit about them today, shall we?"

"How was school today, sweetie?" Carolyn gave her daughter a hug then turned toward the small galley. She picked up the container with their dinner that she'd gotten from the canteen and gathered bowls and forks. She placed everything on the small table and watched as her daughter methodically unpacked her schoolbag. It was a ritual that Carolyn knew was probably a sign of something a bit strange in Becky's brain, but that she found strangely comforting to watch. She wondered if perhaps it was a trait she shared with her daughter, albeit in a less significant way. Regardless, she had convinced herself that unless it began to interfere with her life, her daughter could keep her daily routines without interference.

"School was good," Becky said once her few things were arranged the way she liked. She looked at her mother, eyes wide. "We're learning about the bridge crew."

"Oh," Carolyn said. "That's exciting. You remember your Auntie Celia went to Crew a couple of years ago?"

Becky nodded solemnly. "We don't see Auntie Celia any more."

"No," Carolyn said, "that's just how it is when you become Crew." She felt the old familiar sense of loss come over her and tried to ignore it. "Maybe you'll learn about what Celia is doing on the bridge."

Becky shook her head. "It's history class."

Carolyn portioned out the food, taking care to separate the colours in Becky's bowl. "So, who are you learning about?"

"The first crew," Becky said, spearing a bit of broccoli. "It's part of the unit on the First Heroes."

"Ah," Carolyn said. She had a fluttering feeling in her stomach that she hoped the rich sauce in the stew would quell. She had never liked that term for the initial company of the ship. It had overtones of worship that she found very uncomfortable. But she didn't think she could articulate her objection well enough to talk to Becky's teacher about it. Words were not her speciality—pipes and fittings were. And she couldn't argue that the people who first left old Earth for a destination they would never see were heroes. The veneration just seemed somehow unseemly.

"Today we learned about Nadia Saïd," Becky said, putting her fork down. "She was from an island on old Earth called Australia. Many of the First Heroes were from islands in the Specific Ocean, because of the water getting bigger? We haven't learned about that part yet. Anyway, Nadia Saïd was a farmer in Australia, but she didn't want to stay on old Earth any more. She worked really hard in the training program, learned all kinds of different things and was chosen for the bridge crew! Some of the stories from back then say she could lift people off the ground with one arm!"

Carolyn forced a smile and let Becky recite what she had learned. No matter what she may think about the way the school was teaching history, she couldn't complain about the sense of importance the work was given. She would have preferred them to describe people and their deeds with more accuracy and less embellishment, but the students were only children after all. They liked stories with heroes and magicians, and if it made them appreciate where they came from, well, maybe it didn't hurt to give the lowest ranking member of the initial bridge crew superhuman strength. Surely the kids would grow up and eventually realize that it was just a story.

Becky finally finished recounting her day and Carolyn took the opportunity to talk about what she had done. She couldn't imagine that her seven-year old daughter understood much about what she said, but when she was talking that meant that Becky would eat. Her daughter's reliance on routines was frustrating to people who weren't familiar with her, but it made Carolyn's life easier. When Carolyn wanted Becky to do something in particular, she just had to enact the right ritual. When she saw other mothers fighting to get their kids to behave, Carolyn was grateful for her daughter's quirks.

"All right, children, today I'm going to tell you about the great navigator Yolanda. Do any of you know the story of Yolanda and the spider?"

"Yolanda saw a spider on her way to the ship and used the spider's power to find the web of stars."

"Yes, Juli, that's one of the versions of the spider story. I'm going to tell you a slightly different one.

"It was the day of leaving, the day all of the First Heroes had trained long and hard to see. They left the training facilities on old Earth and walked the long trail to the hatch of the ship. There were people on either side to see them off—family, friends. They knew they would never see the heroes again, but even though that made them sad, they were proud of the great journey these people would be making. The most wondrous journey of all time.

"The crew were the last people in the line to board the ship. They walked slowly toward the hatch, stopping to talk to people along the way, leaving little gifts for people to remember them by. Yolanda was walking toward a friend when she stopped, as if by an invisible force. People around her asked each other what it was, then watched as Yolanda bent down to the ground. She held out her hand and let a small spider climb onto her palm.

"She said to the people, 'I am leaving this place. I will never return. My children will never know the touch of an atmosphere, the heat of a sun. But it is for the people of the future that I go, that we all leave you here. We are not abandoning Earth. We are taking the Earth's children to the stars, to give us all a better chance for the future. And I will take this, one of Earth's tiniest creatures, with us as a reminder of the wonder of this place.' Then she boarded the ship, spider and all."

"Is Yolanda's spider still here?"

"That's a good question, Rachel. Most spiders live only for a few years, and even the ones who live longest only live about twenty years. So it's impossible that any spiders from Earth that came aboard the ship would still be alive today. But that initial spider lives on in its offspring, and the idea that Yolanda's spider represents— the memory of our old home on Earth—that idea is very much still here, don't you think? Yes, Becky?"

"You said this was a story."

"I did."

"So, did it really happen? Did Yolanda really bring a spider on this ship?"

"No one knows, really. Some people think the stories about the First Heroes are true historical facts, but other people think they are metaphors. That means that they are made up stories that describe the truth, without being factually true themselves. But it's not as important whether the events in the stories really happened exactly the way the stories say they did. The important thing is that we learn the message these stories are trying to teach us. So, what do you think the messages are in the story of Yolanda's spider?"

"I think it's great that they teach the next generation about us like we're superheroes." Zell had her feet up on the waste processing tank and sipped from her mug of tea. She made a face. "Though you know who real superheroes would be? Whoever manages to make something hot to drink that doesn't taste like dirt. Ugh." She put the mug down and pushed it away.

"You really think so?" Carolyn asked.

"Yeah," Zell said. "This stuff is disgusting."

"Not the tea. The way they tell these stories like they're maybe almost true. Becky told me that her teacher wouldn't outright say that they're made up. I mean, these are children. They'll believe anything an adult says."

"What's the harm in a little magic?" Zell said. "They grow up soon enough, and reality will get them then. For now, why not let them think people can do anything?"

"I don't know," Carolyn said. "Because it isn't true? And because the truth is better than supernatural abilities for a few. I want Becky to grow up knowing that she is as capable as any of the people that came before her, that we got where we are by working hard, by working together. That it isn't magic, it's human intelligence."

Zell shrugged her broad shoulders. "I'm sure she'll get that."

"Yeah, because I'll tell her," Carolyn said. "But not every mother will. What about those kids?"

"I don't know," Zell said.

"Well, I know," Carolyn said. "I've sent an official request to the Council to have a ruling on the way they are teaching history. I'm hoping we can get rid of all this hero-worship nonsense."

"Gee, Carolyn," Zell said, "why not get rid of *all* worship while you're at it."

"Indeed. Why not?" Carolyn said and her friend and colleague rolled her eyes.

"Well, now that you've solved the religion problem, we better get back to this tank. You got the router ready?"

"Yeah." Carolyn frowned. Disagreeing with Zell made her tense, but she didn't have anyone else to talk to. Outside work, she spent all her time with Becky. She fitted the tool to the maintenance duct and got to work.

When Carolyn got to her quarters, they were empty. Becky would be home any minute, though—she was a punctual child. Carolyn sat in her usual chair, thinking. She was still there when the door slid open and Becky came in.

"Hi, mom," she said, hoisting her bag up on to the table. She sat in her chair and began to unpack.

"Hi, sweetie," Carolyn said, not getting up. She let Becky lay out her school supplies. When the little girl was done, she stayed at the table, staring across to the seat Carolyn usually occupied at this time. She made no sign to move.

"Sweetie," Carolyn said, "can you come over here? I'd like to talk with you."

"But it's suppertime." Becky said, unmoving.

"I know it is, but I'd like to talk."

"Food first, then we talk," Becky said, her voice beginning to quaver a little. Carolyn sighed and got up. She wanted to get this over with, before she forgot the careful phrasings she'd planned. But she knew her daughter. *Food first, then we talk.* There could be no other way of doing things without a struggle. And Carolyn wanted Becky to listen to what she had to say, not spend all her energy on trying to make a chaotic situation more orderly.

"Okay," she said, heating up some food in the small bulkhead-mounted unit.

"We learned about multiplication today." Becky said the long word slowly, each syllable carefully enunciated, but correctly. "It's like stacking things in a grid. To make four across and three down you need twelve things."

"Very good," Carolyn said, as the oven bleeped. She opened the hatch and savoury steam escaped. Her stomach rumbled. Becky was probably right about eating first, after all.

She dished out the food and Becky told her more about the math lesson. Of course, Carolyn wanted to think her daughter was bright and talented, but it really did seem as though Becky had a head for numbers. She wasn't really surprised—math was Celia's strength, too, and Becky's fondness for symmetry and order always reminded Carolyn of geometry.

Becky's account of her day petered out and Carolyn took her own turn. "Have you learned about the old human custom of religion yet?" she asked and Becky, mouth full of food, shook her head. "It's something that used to be important to many people on old Earth. They told stories about the creation of the land and the sky, stories about important people, stories about why things happened in the natural world. The stories made people feel like they understood a world which was confusing and often frightening. They helped people find meaning in their lives."

Becky chewed, then said, "Like the stories of the First Heroes. My teacher called them..." she closed her eyes, as she often did when trying to remember something, "metaphors."

"Exactly," Carolyn said, letting a long breath out. "But different groups of people had different stories, and they fought about which were right. And people who were in charge began to use those stories as a way to make the rest of the people do whatever they wanted. The stories didn't stop being useful, but they did have bad sides, too."

"Why would people fight about the stories? If they weren't really true?"

"Well, some people thought they were true. But what I'm trying to tell you is that the stories are important, even when we know they are metaphors. They still make us feel particular ways about the people and things they talk about. And I want you to know that it's okay to decide for yourself what think about the stories you hear, not to just accept what other people tell you they mean. Do you understand?"

Becky nodded. "I think so." She ate the last of her meal, then carefully laid the fork at what Carolyn knew to be a 45° angle on the plate. It wouldn't be long before Becky knew that, too. "Is it all right if I go and think about Yolanda's Spider now?"

Carolyn smiled. "That is definitely all right." She picked up the plates, careful not to disturb Becky's arrangement. Her daughter's rituals gave her days order and meaning, and Carolyn knew how desperately Becky clung to those tiny moments of control. They were her own private mythology that she could probably never explain, and Carolyn just hoped that one day Becky would think about them as carefully as she was most certainly now thinking about stories from generations gone by.

143

"Call me Steve."

Keith looked over, unsure what this meant. "Uh, okay," he said. "You want to talk about it?"

"Naw," she said, "I'm not changing anything else. I just don't like being pigeon-holed into the binary, you know?"

He didn't know, but he nodded anyway. Stephanie—*Steve*, he corrected himself—was always saying things he didn't understand. It was part of her charm. They were sitting in the darkest corner of the library, as they did most days after school. Keith needed the library time to study. He was struggling with the advanced mathematics course and he knew that if he didn't complete the material in the 90th percentile, he'd never have a chance at the Academy entrance exam. Still, he set his tablet aside and waited to see if Steve had anything else to add to this nomenclature development.

She didn't say anything for a moment and Keith didn't know what to contribute to the conversation. Despite what she'd said, he wondered if Steve was planning to transition. She had always been what Keith's mom called a tomboy, and in the last year she'd given up all trappings of stereotypical femininity. Once she'd started showing up to school wearing an old, discarded spacesuit, Keith had really wondered what was going on in her head.

He'd tried to talk about it once. "You ever think that things didn't turn out, you know," he fumbled for the right way to put it, "typically?" He peeked up at her from behind a problem about zero-g propulsion. "With your body, or your DNA or something?"

Stephanie, as she'd still called herself then, put down her stylus and frowned. Keith looked over at her tablet and saw a bunch of strange squiggles he didn't understand. There was a title in text, though, that read *Study in E flat*. He didn't know what that meant, either. "I don't think so," Stephanie answered after obviously giving the question some thought. "Why?"

Keith shrugged and tried to fight the flush creeping across his face. "Dunno," he mumbled and went back to staring at the physics problem.

"Oh, god," Stephanie said and pulled the tablet from his grasp. "I am such an idiot. I'm sorry, Keith, I didn't realize." She moved over to face him directly and Keith felt his heart rate increase. He didn't understand why in the past few years being with Stephanie had become so... strange. He knew all about men and women and adolescence and hormones, but this just seemed ridiculous. He'd known Stephanie almost since he was born. And he was pretty sure he didn't like her like that. Fairly sure.

"What?" he asked, tamping down the panic and thrill that were competing for mindshare.

"Are you having, you know, *feelings*?" she asked, her voice low and intense.

Keith blinked at her. He couldn't imagine why she would think that he... oh. She thought he was trying to feel her out, see how she would react, so he could confess some major teenage secret. As if there were anything weird about him that could compete with her everyday self.

He shook his head. "No. I'm still boring. I just thought, maybe you... Never mind." He let his voice trail off, then noticed a distant point in space that became immediately fascinating.

"Oh," she said and Keith swore he could detect a hint of embarrassment in her voice. It couldn't be, though. Nothing fazed Stephanie. She was invincible.

They never talked about it again. Not until that afternoon, when they'd been talking about the ship-wide track tournament, and apropos of nothing she'd asked him to call her Steve.

"Did your mom get weird when she and my mom split up?" Steve asked Keith. They sat on the edge of the reservoir, feet dangling in the water. Keith couldn't help noticing that Steve had done something to her chest. She was wearing a loose top and swim shorts, like about half the kids at the water's edge. But Keith was certain that she used to be a lot curvier than she now seemed to be. He tried not to let her catch him looking.

"Yeah," he answered and threw a pebble into the water. "I know they said it was mutual, just one of those things, but Mom seemed pretty sad for a long time after."

Steve nodded and stared out over the water. Keith had decided that she must be done with the conversation when she said, "Mine, too." She kicked her feet, sending splashes of water into the air. Keith watched the droplets hover for a microsecond before floating back down to the surface of the water. It made him think of the time he'd taken a trip to the zero-gravity level in the centre of the ship, how he'd bounced through the room as if he were on a trampoline. He'd been young enough then to be able to just have fun. Now, he'd be too worried about what he looked like, if people would think he was dumb for finding jumping around in weightlessness entertaining.

He knew swimming was acceptable fun, though, so stood. He could feel a warm breeze on his back, the recyclers pushing out cleaned air from the ducts behind him. "Come on," he said and leapt off the edge of the platform. He tucked his thin body into a ball and hit the water with a splash that sent a column of water straight up. As it came back down, it spread out and covered Steve in a cascade of drops.

"Keith!" she squealed and he smiled. That sounded like the Stephanie he remembered. She stood and dove into the water head first, her body an arrow aimed at his heart. She tackled him underwater and they wrestled until they couldn't breathe, then they floated on their backs looking up at the lights and ductwork of the ceiling.

"It just doesn't seem worth it," she said and Keith knew she wasn't just talking about their parents. She was talking about all couples. She was talking about love.

Neither Keith nor Steve knew it at the time, but when their mothers began to become close, they almost killed the relationship before it began. Keith found out years later, long after the relationship ended. He'd started paying more attention to the love stories than the adventure and mystery ones. It was about this time that it started being, not exactly *awkward* with Stephanie, but different. He knew enough to know that it was mostly just his body chemistry changing, but that didn't make him feel any better about it.

"When you and Marie-Claire became a couple," he asked his mother one evening, "how did you know? I mean, how did you know you liked her like that?" He hated the way he sounded, as if he were just another dumb twelve-year-old. But he didn't know how else to ask, and it wasn't as if talking about his mother's former partner who just happened to be his best friend's mom was easy.

His mother had sighed, but not the exasperated sigh he feared. It was more a dreamy, remembering sigh, which made Keith feel both more and less uncomfortable. "I remember when I was about your age," she said, "asking my mother about love. 'How do you know if you're really in love?' I asked. She told me that there was no way to explain it, you just know." She looked at Keith and smiled. "It was the most useless thing I'd ever heard, and I promised myself then and there that I'd never answer a question like that." She paused and stared at a spot on the wall of their quarters. "The trouble is, it's hard to explain. And probably different for everyone, anyway. But I'll try.

"You know Marie-Claire and I were friends for a long time first?" Keith nodded. Of course, his mother and Marie-Claire had been apprentices at the same time and they often worked together. They got pregnant in the same year and they'd spent all their free time together with their new babies. Keith and Stephanie were nearly as close as siblings. But sometime when the kids were just starting school, something had changed. "I don't know exactly what happened for her, but I think I always loved M-C. She was the most fun person I knew and anytime I did anything, she was the first person I wanted to share it with. But I never thought of her as a romantic partner, because, well, women aren't really my thing." Keith could see that his mother was nearly as embarrassed talking about this with him as he was hearing it. But he couldn't get out of this conversation now, and the awfulness of it all somehow made it all the more compelling.

"So, what happened?" he asked.

His mother shrugged and tried to cover up her nervous laugh with a cough. "Maybe I just got older, maybe I realized that there's more to life than physical attraction. Maybe my tastes changed, I don't really know. It felt kind of like a switch was thrown somewhere inside me. One day, she was just my buddy M-C. The next day..." She couldn't cover the crimson flush that rose up her cheeks. "The next day I wanted something more." She sighed. "I know this isn't a good answer, Keith. It's just a lot more words to say, 'you'll know love when you find it,' I guess." She stood and walked into the small galley and drew a glass of water.

"We were really worried about how it would affect you and Stephanie," she said, still facing the faucet. "We knew there was no pretending that nothing had changed, and we also knew that the odds of us staying together forever were slim. M-C really wasn't sure —I had to lobby hard to get her to agree to even try." She laughed then, but it sounded like sadness rather than mirth. She didn't turn around and Keith guessed that she was crying again.

"Was it worth it?" He finally asked the question he really needed answered.

He saw his mother take a deep breath and when she turned he could see that her eyes were red, but the smile on her face was genuine. "Absolutely," she said.

Keith walked out of his classroom grinning. Amal, his physics teacher, had just confirmed Keith's final grade. "I did it," he said, catching up with Steve as she was leaving her own language class, "91st percentile!"

"Good job, buddy," she said and grinned at him. "I knew you'd pull it off. You're going to make a great engineer."

"We both will," Keith said and frowned as Steve shrugged. "Come on, I know you've got the marks."

"Yeah," she said, "I just don't know if it's what I want to do."

"What are you saying?" Keith stopped and reached his hand out to Steve's shoulder. He grabbed her and she stopped walking and turned to face him.

"Engineering is your thing," she said. "You're going to be great at it, too. I... I don't know. There's a lot I don't know, okay? Just, don't push me right now." She brushed past him and walked off, everything in her body language telling Keith not to follow her. He followed her.

"But you're a natural," he said, his long legs catching up to her easily. "We'd go to the Academy, study together, maybe even work together later. How can you just throw that all away?" He reached out for her again, but this time she batted his hand away and wheeled around to look at him.

"Things change, Keith," she said, her eyes narrowing. "Can't you see that? Just leave it alone for now. I mean it." She turned and walked away and this time Keith let her go.

What was happening to them?

They didn't talk for more than ten days. Keith couldn't remember if they'd ever gone so long without speaking. He was starting to think that he'd done something irrevocable, that she would never talk to him again. His pain was obvious.

"What's going on, sweetheart?" his mother asked. "Did something happen between you and Stephanie?"

"It's Steve now," Keith muttered.

"Oh," his mother said, her eyebrows rising. "Is she... uh, is he...?"

"She hasn't changed. That's not the problem," Keith spat out, wondering if he was telling the truth. "It's just a name. You know her, she's always got to be different."

His mother looked at him and Keith could feel her trying to figure out what to say. "Sometimes," she said, her voice soft, "friends go through different stages of closeness. This is a big time for both of you—leaving school, going on to choose a path in life. Soon Steph— Steve will have to think about children, you too, maybe. It's a crazy time right now. It's no surprise that things aren't exactly the same as they've always been with you two."

"Yeah," Keith said and peeked at his mother through his hair. He couldn't tell if she really believed what she was saying, but he wanted to believe it.

Later that night, he wasn't sleeping and he heard his mother on the comms with Marie-Claire. He couldn't hear Steve's mom's side of the conversation, but his own mother wasn't as quiet as she thought she was. He propped the door to his bedroom open and sat against the wall, straining to hear.

"... he's terribly upset about whatever it is. It's as if they've split up ... No, he didn't tell me that anything specific happened ... She's moping around, too? ... I don't envy kids these days ... I know ... You'd think it would be easier to tell them that they're only making themselves miserable ... Yes, I know they have to go through it themselves, I just wish ... Yes, you, too."

Keith slipped his door closed and lay on top of his bed. So Steve was miserable, too. Why did that not make him feel any better?

She called him a few days before the end of school ceremony. "I was just going to ask if you were going to the party," she said over the comms. She didn't look into the camera, and Keith worried for a moment that she was going to tell him something terrible. "But we really need to talk, I guess," she finished.

"Yeah," Keith said, his stomach clenched. "You want to meet at the garden or something?"

Steve nodded and looked up. Her eyes were red, not like she'd been crying, but as if she hadn't slept well in a few days. "Yeah, the autumn garden's nice. Can you be there in thirty minutes?"

I would drop anything, he thought. I'd find a way to move the stars if I had to. "Sure," he said aloud.

She was there when he arrived. He walked over to where she sat under a large tree. Its leaves were turning and there was a small carpet of yellow and orange around the base of the trunk. She sat in a clearing and was turning a bright orange leaf over in her hand. Keith's step cracked a branch and she looked up. Keith saw something familiar and wonderful in her face and his throat constricted. Is this it? Is this just knowing when it's real?

"Hey," he said and walked over to Steve. "Can I sit?"

"Of course," she said and laughed a little. It sounded forced.

"Are we okay?" Keith blurted. "I don't know what I did, but I'm sorry. I just... I just don't want..."

She put her hand lightly on his arm and he felt his skin almost burn at her touch. "We're okay," she said. "At least, we are as far as I'm concerned." She squeezed lightly, then took her hand back. She looked away from him and Keith followed the path of her gaze. The trees were beautiful in this room, he thought. He wondered if he'd ever noticed that before.

"I know I've been weird," Steve began, "weird even for me." She laughed and this time it sounded real.

"Kind of," Keith said.

"It's so embarrassing," she said, "so typical. End of school rolls around and I go all 'got to find my authentic self' on you." She shook her head. "I feel like such a loser, but what can I say? You get told you have to decide what you want to spend your life doing, it makes you think."

"Yeah, it does," Keith said. "I don't think that makes you a loser."

Steve punched him in the arm. "Like you'd know," she said but she was smiling. "Anyway, I figured out that I didn't like who I was. Who everyone was trying to make me be, I guess. I don't want to be an engineer, Keith. I know that's not what you or anyone else expects, but it's the way it is. And since it's the only thing I actually can control right now, I'm making sure I don't get stuck in a job I don't love." She looked away and all trace of lightness left her. "Especially since I can't help the rest of it."

"The rest of what?" Keith asked.

"Everything! Life, me, being who I am." She ran her hands over her head, the short hair unaffected by the touch. Keith waited. "I know it's out of my control," she said, "but, god, I do not want to be a mother. But I don't want to be a man, either. So what am I supposed to do?"

"I..." Keith didn't know what to say. It had never occurred to him that his friend would be worried about things like that. He had always hoped he would one day get to be a parent—not just an anonymous donor, but actually around for his children, like his mother was for him. But he knew it was a choice at best, the luck of the draw at worst. For him, it was optional. He'd never even thought about what it would be like for a woman, what it would be like for her.

"You know I'm not like everyone else," Steve said. "I've never been like any of the other girls and I'm not a boy, so where do I fit in? I don't and that's fine but it's not easy and..." She paused to take a breath and Keith leaned over and put his arm around her shoulder. He figured she'd probably shrug it off but was surprised when she leaned into his embrace.

"Thanks," she said, her voice muffled into his shirt. "Sorry I'm breaking down on you, here."

"It's okay," he said. "I had no idea you felt so... complicated. You've always just been, well, *you*."

She laughed then and looked up at him. "Yeah," she said. "I think it's just everything all at once, you know. All the pressure to go to the Academy is what did it in the end. I feel like I've spent my whole life fighting what everyone expects of me, only to end up with just another set of expectations. 'Stephanie isn't like the other girls, but it's okay because she's a natural with numbers.' Well, I don't love numbers."

"So, what do you love?" Keith asked.

"I want to write music," she said, pulling away from him but leaving her hand in his. "I want to make beautiful noise that makes people remember there's more to the universe than this tin can."

"Well," Keith said, "go do it, then. I'm the one who needs the system to make it through. You're smart enough to do whatever you want."

Steve looked at him. "You really think that, don't you?"

"Sure," Keith said. "Maybe it doesn't feel like it to you, but you've been going your own way all along. No reason to stop now."

"Oh, sure," Steve said, "like I'll just give up my assigned place at the Academy, run off and live in the trees, writing symphonies in the dirt. No one will let me do that."

"There must be a way," Keith said. "Isn't there a music school or something?"

Steve smiled but it was without any warmth. "Yeah, but it's just a half-time course on the comms. Almost everyone there is post-natal, let alone careered. I looked into it—I even got an acceptance, but I'll need a job. And who's going to hire me in a trade right out of school, when it's public knowledge that I got into the Academy?"

"Don't look at me," Keith said. "You're the brain." She punched him on the shoulder then leaned her back into the bruise.

"It's so beautiful here," she said. "I kind of wish I really could just live here."

"You could probably get away with it for a couple of days."

"Don't tempt me," she said and sighed. "So, are you going to the party or what?"

"You really did want to ask that after all?"

"Sure," she said. "I mean, I kind of want to go, but I'm not going if you're not going."

"Of course I'll go," Keith said, an idea forming in his mind.

Someone had gotten a hold of the most recent songs from the Yellow Sector band *A Heart, Agape* and was blasting them through a group of inflatable speakers. The cacophonous sound was almost painful, but Keith knew it was what was popular. "That stuff is dreadful," he said.

"Yeah, it's atonal," Steve said, "but there's pretty complex harmonics under it all, if you can ignore the top notes." He looked at Steve out of the corner of his eye and grinned. She was dressed in some kind of bizarre combination of mechanics coveralls with a mesh top underneath. Keith could see that instead of a bra or undershirt she'd wrapped a band around her chest, which explained the body change he'd noticed in her. The whole outfit looked surprisingly okay, he thought.

It seemed like the entire class was there. The end of school party was something of a legend. No one was supposed to talk about what happened, but the rumours were seemingly endless. It was an open secret that many partnerships got their start at the big party, and that a few budding ones ended in flames. No matter what kind of student a kid had been, the party was a symbolic end to one part of life and a beginning to another.

"It's our last chance at fun," Steve said as they walked over to the table laid out with snacks and drinks. She picked up a tiny slice of flatbread with a smear of green on it and popped it into her mouth. "That's why they don't shut this down. They know that if we have one day to get it all out of our systems, it'll be a lot easier to just accept our fate and go on to be productive members of society."

Keith knew Steve was being overly dramatic, but he also knew she was more right than wrong. She didn't seem bitter about it, though, and that surprised him.

"You're a lot more sanguine about the whole event now than you were a few days ago," he said. Steve just shrugged.

"There are problems you can do something about and problems you can't. The first step to a solution is to determine which is which."

Keith nodded and grabbed two glasses of a suspicious-looking pink liquid. "Come on," he said, jerking his head in the direction of a set of climbing apparatus made of rope. "Let's go hang out over there. I've got a plan."

They wove their way through groups of adolescents, most of whom were from other areas of the ship. On the way, they recognized a knot of their classmates, who uncharacteristically waved them over.

"Hey, Keith, Stephanie, great party, isn't it?" Keith recognized the gregarious voice of Melinda Watt. He was certain she had never spoken two words to him previously.

"Sure," Steve said, "stellar. You must be excited to be moving on from school."

"I know," Melinda said, "I can't wait to be on my own. Training, a position, then finally quarters of my own." She looked between Keith and Steve. "You two are so lucky, going to the Academy. You'll get away from home that much sooner, am I right?"

"I guess," Steve said taking a sip of her drink and grimacing. Melinda elbowed her in the ribs and Steve sputtered.

"Are they going to let you two room together?" she said, and it sounded like she was trying for a whisper.

"I dunno," Keith said, looking at Melinda strangely. "Why would they?"

"Come on," Melinda said. "Everyone knows about you two. Lots of people partner right out of school, why shouldn't they let you share quarters?"

Steve sighed. "We're not..." she began but Keith interrupted her.

"We'll ask," he said, shooting Steve a 'shut-up-I'll-explain-later' glare. "Anyway, good to see you Melinda." He grabbed Steve's non-drink arm and dragged her away before she could say anything else.

"What the stars was that?" she said once they'd gotten out of earshot.

"Just laying the foundation," Keith said. "Come on, let's climb up where people won't overhear."

"You want to what?" Steve said, the look in her eyes scaring Keith a little. He'd known that he was taking a big chance suggesting this, but it also seemed like the best possible plan. For both of them.

"Think about it," he said. "You'd have a place to live, you'd get leave from school and then you could do the music course. I know they wouldn't make you go back to the Academy after—it's part of the whole Next Generation First program. As soon as a doctor confirms it, you'd be set."

"I cannot believe you are seriously suggesting this," Steve said. "You know how I feel about... this whole thing."

"Yeah," Keith said and looked out over the grounds below. There were at least a thousand bodies down there, all of them propelled by their hopes and fantasies and fears about their futures. He knew that a good fraction of them probably felt like Steve—trapped by circumstance, duty and legislation. He also knew that he was lucky—what he wanted from life was acceptable, normal, easy.

"Besides," he said turning back to look at her. "You're going to have to do it eventually. Unless you, you know..." he gestured at her body and raised an eyebrow.

She looked at him, her eyes wide. He wondered if he had really done it this time, really gone so far that she wouldn't be able to still be his friend after this. He realized he was holding his breath.

"You really think it would work?" she asked, her voice so quiet he wouldn't have heard her if she hadn't been the focus of all of his attentions.

"Yes," he said, "I really do. But we'd have to start making it look real." He dropped his eyes. "I thought it would be harder to convince people that we were, you know..." He blushed. "But I guess not." He glanced over to Steve and saw a smile start to peek out across her face.

"You seriously didn't know that everyone thinks you're my boyfriend?" she said, laughing aloud now. "God, you're an idiot sometimes."

"But this time?"

She pursed her lips in thought then shook her head once. "No. This time you're not an idiot."

"I've found us a doctor who has agreed to do the procedure without asking too many questions," Keith said as he ladled out bowls of thick stew.

"Good work," Steve said, her tablet covered in equations and diagrams. "And I've finished your quantum fluctuations assignment, but this is the last time. I'm telling you, I don't want to be an engineer, and I especially don't want to be an engineer whose work all gets credited to you."

"I know, I'm sorry," Keith said, sitting at the table in their quarters. He looked across at Steve and was amazed at how easy the transition to partners had gone. "But if you went to the clinics alone they'd just hook you up with a donor. It has to be me, you know that."

"I know," Steve said, her voice softening. "I was just being an ass." She grinned and Keith was reminded of how she'd looked before they were even in school, playing some game she'd devised.

"Speaking of which, you're only going to be in the 60th percentile on that assignment."

"What?"

Steve shrugged. "You need some motivation to keep studying, or you'll never learn this stuff."

"Sometimes I wonder why I put up with you," he said and they both laughed. "But seriously, they can do it in the clinic. I go in first and..." He blushed—that hadn't changed even though they'd been living together for over a year. "Then you need to go within a couple of days." He looked at Steve who had stopped eating.

"You ready for this?" he asked.

She shook her head. "No," she said, "but I never will be. Now is as good a time as any for that part of it, and if I want to move on from the Academy, the sooner the better. But, Keith," she leaned across the table and took his hand. It wasn't something that happened often, so he knew it was important. "Are you ready?"

He took a breath. "Yes," he said. "I think so."

"Okay then," Steve squeezed his hand briefly, then let go and went back to her meal. "Make the appointments."

He was tiny and healthy and they called him Ryan. Keith was surprised how much the child amused Steve, but she was right about her maternal instincts. Left to her, Ryan would be ignored when he stopped being entertaining. But Keith couldn't have been happier than when he was with the baby.

As soon as it was confirmed that she was pregnant, Steve dropped out of the Academy. She started the music classes and spent much of her day with her tablet. She'd even managed to get a hold of a keyboard attachment for next to nothing and Keith finally got to hear what she heard in her mind. It was wonderful.

Everyone they knew said that pregnancy changed her—she blossomed, they said. Only Keith knew better.

He took a term's parental leave from the Academy when Ryan was born, then returned to school part-time. It was still a struggle, but Steve being happy made everything in their small quarters better. And while she may not have wanted to work as an engineer, she was always willing to help Keith. Their days were spent with her writing music, Keith taking care of Ryan and Steve quizzing him on his classes.

The years passed, Keith graduated and went to work for the hydroponics lab. They moved halfway round the ship—a grand adventure for Ryan, larger quarters and closer proximity to the cultural centres. Keith thought they were happy.

He had dropped Ryan off at the school and walked back to their quarters, his mind on the redesign for the fruit greenhouse. He made a notation on his tablet as he approached the door to his quarters when an unfamiliar sound brought him out of his thoughts. It sounded like a sob, but not the quick-to-start, quick-to-end cry of a child. This had the feel of something that was escaping unbidden by its vessel, as if it were a lifeform of its own and was finally being released from an unwanted captivity. He wondered idly where it was coming from then realized almost simultaneously that it emanated from his own quarters. Strangely, he initially wondered who could possibly be in there. Only later did he realize that in all the years of their friendship, this was the first time he had heard Steve cry.

He found her in bed, under the covers even though it was well into the day. Her weeping had drowned out the sounds of his arrival and he knew she didn't realize that he was there. He knew, also, that she would be mortified if she knew that he had witnessed this.

He padded softly out of the room, grabbed the notes he'd forgotten—the reason he had returned to their quarters unexpectedly— and slipped back into the corridor. Once he'd escaped, the full force of Steve's evident despair hit him. It was as if all his breath were violently sucked from his body and he felt tears of his own prick his eyes. He slid down the wall next to the door and tried to understand what could possibly make her so unhappy.

After, Keith paid close attention to Steve every day, but he could never catch her doing or saying anything which would give him an opportunity to broach the subject of her happiness. He began to wonder if he'd imagined it, but knew that it was not a scene he could ever had created. His image of Steve just didn't include anything like this.

Ryan was in his room, as usual, when Steve came home from a rehearsal. The Starboard Symphony was performing one of her sonatas in their upcoming recital and Steve had been actively involved in the production. It was to be the most prestigious showcase of her work so far and Keith was excited for her. She, however, seemed to be more stressed than proud.

She dropped her tablet on the table and sank into a chair. "Tough rehearsal?" Keith asked.

Steve rubbed her eyes. "Not really," she answered. "It's all just... a lot of work."

"It's what you've always wanted, though," Keith said. "Since when are you afraid of work?"

"I'm not," she said, looking up at him, then looking away quickly.

Keith looked over toward Ryan's room and saw that the boy was deeply immersed in whatever he was doing. Ryan had inherited Keith's seriousness and Steve's quickness to learn, so he was a favourite among his teachers. He happily spent hours in his room with his tablet—reading, playing complex games, sketching. Keith sometimes wished that his child wanted his attention a little more, but he knew that he was lucky. He knew he was, in fact, the luckiest person he knew. He took a breath.

"So then, what's wrong?" he asked, his voice soft but serious. He sat down next to Steve. "Talk to me."

"I..." she said, then looked away again. "I feel awful, Keith. But it's too late, I don't know how to fix it. I'm... I'm so sorry."

"Sorry for what?" he asked and she turned to look at him. He swore he could see tears in her eyes, but her voice never wavered.

"For ruining your life. For wrecking your chance for happiness, for... a normal life. A normal..." She looked around their quarters. "A normal family."

Keith was stunned. He didn't say anything for several seconds.

"Has something happened?" he asked carefully. "Is there someone else?" He tried to keep his voice level.

"Me?" Steve asked, a look of surprise on her face. "No, of course not. You know I'm not... interested in... that."

"Okay," Keith said, "so what's the problem, then? Have I done something wrong?"

"No," she said and her voice had a plaintive quality that Keith found disturbing. "In all the universe, no. I'm happy—perfectly happy. I have the perfect life—work I love, hanging out with my best friend all the time, who takes care of everything. But that's exactly the problem." She looked at Keith and appeared to be making a decision. "You have always done everything for me. You let me live with you, pretended to be my partner, let me use you to get pregnant, then did so much more than your share for Ryan. I've used you, Keith, and it's totally unfair. You should be able to find a partner who will, you know, do those things that partners do. You deserve someone better than me, Keith. But with Ryan..." Her eyes drifted over to the boy's room and Keith heard something in her throat catch. "Now it's too late. At least for a few years. I'm so sorry, Keith. I was selfish and I let you give up so much for me and now I can't fix it."

She looked down at her lap and Keith was afraid that she would start crying in earnest now. But he was so angry that he couldn't be bothered to care about that.

"I can't believe you actually think that," he said, his voice trembling. He could feel the beat of his heart throughout his body, making him quiver. "You're my best friend, I love you, and I would do a lot for you," he said holding her gaze, "but if you think this is just for *you*... You really haven't been paying attention to me, have you?"

"I don't understand," Steve said.

"You think I've given something up to be with you," Keith said, "you think I want to live like everyone else and you're the only one who wants a different life? Well, I didn't ask you to live with me, ask you to have a child with me, ask you to be my partner, as a favour to you. It was what *I* wanted. It *is* what I want."

"But," Steve said, a flush starting to colour her cheeks, "we're not really partners."

"Oh, yes, we are," Keith said. "Fucking doesn't make you some-one's partner. Working together, making a home and a life together, that's what makes people a family. And that's what we are." He stared at her, the rest of the room vanishing as the adrenaline narrowed his vision.

"You mean that," she said, no hint of a question in her voice. He nodded. Time passed, seconds probably. To Keith, it felt like an entire universe could have been born, expanded, contracted and died. Finally, Steve broke into a grin and a belly laugh escaped her lips.

"I've never heard you say 'fuck' before," she said, still laughing. It broke the spell on Keith and he began to laugh, too.

"Mom," Ryan said, and Keith turned to see him standing in the doorway of his room. "Are you fighting?"

"No, honey," Steve said, smiling. "Your dad was just explaining something to me. Sometimes I can be a little slow." She reached over and took Keith's hand, squeezed for a nanosecond, then let it go. Ryan frowned but then nodded solemnly.

"Okay," he said. "Andra's parent fight a lot. Nancy's too."

Keith caught Steve's eye and it was like looking back in time, at the friend he knew now that he'd loved his whole life. And he knew that even if no one else understood their relationship, this was it, the real thing.

"Well," he said, "we're not like other parents."

Ryan walked over to them, climbed up on Keith's knee and looked back and forth between them both. "Good," he said.

A superstitious people would say
"We have been blessed"
"Fortune has smiled upon us"
Revering the gods of stories

We instead praise careful planning
intelligence and industry
They are the new gods
Who dwell beside us on our journey

"O, industrious comrades of the past,"
I cry when my mind is weary of the vast unchanging horizon
And my body aches from the creak and sway of the hull
"Be with me now,
That we might make this endless voyage
A song of spirit as well as body."

PART THREE
FORWARD THRUST

Oki was in her usual position: feet up on the console, chair leaned back, reading. This time it was a translation of *The Arabian Nights*, but she wasn't particular. She would read pretty much anything. She had a system—she would read a couple of minutes, scan the screens to make sure nothing had gone screwy, then read some more. Every watch, every day, always the same. She was very well-read.

She heard the sound of someone entering the bridge, but didn't bother to look up from her tablet. It was about the right time for Jenn to come on watch and they'd long since bothered with pleasantries. Why talk if there's nothing to say? She finished her section and put down her handheld. She raised her arms over her head as the chair sprang forward, planted her feet on the deck and stretched. She tilted her head from side to side, and heard her neck crack. It felt good. She stood and saw Jenn at her station, going over the charts. The other woman didn't look up as Oki walked off the bridge and stepped down the ladder toward her quarters.

It was about the middle of her shift the next day, when Oki was startled by a voice from the companionway. "Have your heard the news?" It was Jenn; it wasn't time for her watch and she was talking as she climbed the stairs. Oki dropped her handheld and sprang out of her chair.

"What?" she asked, curiosity, fear and annoyance competing for dominance. "Is there a problem?"

She could just see Jenn's head poke up in the companionway and had to wait an agonizing second before the woman was on the bridge deck proper. She didn't look like whatever it was was life-threatening, so Oki let the fear go.

"Maybe," Jenn said. "We're getting a new crew member."

This wasn't news to Oki. Captain Selani was nearly a hundred years old, and while there were no indications that there was anything wrong with her mind, she had been talking retirement for a few years already. They all knew that soon Ship's Mate Ana Lio would become captain and someone else would join the crew as the mate. This wasn't news. "So?" Oki said, frowning.

"So," Jenn said. "It's a man."

Oki had a vague memory of the captain and Naomi having a conversation about boy babies. It was years ago, and she hadn't cared about it at the time. She left Society and became Crew for similar reasons to the rest of them on the bridge—not a one of them fit in with the expectations and requirements for most of the people aboard the *White Cloud*, the complete lack of interest in having a family being a basic necessity for a life as Crew. The only reason Oki even remembered that the conversation had occurred was that at the time she wondered why they cared. Bits and pieces of the memory filtered back now.

"It seems too soon to me," Naomi had said. "We're only a few generations out. There must be plenty of seed stock left. This is unnecessary and will create no end of problems, I know it."

"I'm not entirely sure what the fuss is all about," the captain said. "People are people and it's not like they'd be treated any different. There are plenty of people who transition now anyway. Before I was Crew, one of the people in the quarters next door was a man. It was fine."

"That's not the same," Naomi said, and that was about when Oki stopped listening. Gender and sex baffled her, even in stories. She understood the literary device of desire and longing that romance created, and the sense of difference between men and women, but they were both as foreign as mountains and rivers and deserts.

She pulled her attention back to the present, and sat down. "So, they started having male children?"

Jenn nodded. "A while back. It didn't seem important—I mean, it never occurred to me that one of them would end up here. I mean..." she looked around the bridge. "It's always just been us."

Oki thought about what Jenn was saying. She listened to the words, but also to the words she didn't say, the silences, the pauses, the ideas in between the words. She watched Jenn's face, her body. Honestly, Oki usually didn't pay much attention to her crewmates, but when she did pay attention, she really paid attention. "You're afraid," she said, finally, after analyzing Jenn's statement. "Why?"

Jenn looked down and a flush rose in her face. "I don't know," she said, and Oki had to strain to hear her even though they were quite close and the bridge wasn't loud. "He'll be... different."

"You must have encountered a man before," Oki said.

Jenn shrugged her shoulders. "This isn't the same thing. Natural-born males—their bodies... they aren't like us, Oki. You must know, must have read about it."

Oki shrugged. "The Committee wouldn't send someone who can't handle crew life."

Jenn didn't look convinced, but she didn't argue. After all, Oki thought, what would be the point? The existing crew had never had a say in choosing a new member before, it didn't seem likely that would change now. And, of course, there had to be a first time for everything.

"I'm sure you've all heard the news by now," the captain said, her hands clinging to the mug siting in front of her. Oki sometimes wondered why Teena Selani had been chosen as captain. She had always seemed uncomfortable in a group, had no natural leadership qualities that Oki could recognize. Under her watch the crew rarely held the kind of meeting where all would gather in one place—Captain Selani seemed to prefer to speak one-on-one or to catch two crew members at watch change if they needed to talk.

But the same day that Jenn had interrupted Oki's watch to tell her the news, Captain Selani had called for all hands on deck. The six of them crowded on to the bridge, most of them leaning against bulkheads or half-seated on the ledge of a console. "I'll be retiring at the end of this year, and that means a new crew member has been chosen. His name is Matthew Peelu. He was one of the first generation of biologically born males on board the ship. He will be joining us in two weeks."

No one said a word. Oki looked around the semi-circular space at the faces of her crewmates. The captain had been right—they had all heard the rumour before she called the meeting, but Oki could tell that a few of them hadn't believed it. Cat's face was a mask of neutrality, which Oki knew meant that she was holding back some kind of strong emotion. At the other end of the spectrum, Ana looked openly disgusted, but said nothing. She must have already said her piece privately to the captain before the meeting. As the new captain, she would have to interact most closely with the new mate.

Evie was the first to say something. "He must be young; there weren't any boy babies when I was in Society." Evie was the most recent crew member to join, and at just over fifty years old, was the youngest as well.

The captain nodded. "He is. Very young. Just in his twenties." This *was* news, and there were gasps around the room.

"I don't understand," Cat said. "Has anyone that young ever become Crew before?"

The captain nodded. "It's not as unusual as it seems," she said.

"The first crew, obviously, were young. Leaving one's homeworld is, after all, an adventure for youth. But there have been others." She sipped from her mug and looked around the bridge. Her brown eyes lit on each person in turn, and Oki felt something very much like an almost familial concern from the old woman. It gave her the warm feeling in her chest that she imagined when she read stories about love.

"I hope that none of you is under the misapprehension that the main reason any of us were chosen for Crew was a special ability with stellar cartography or engine calibration." There were flushed faces and avoided glances, but the captain's smile held no trace of cruelty. "This is a starship. We have more than our share of bright minds with nothing more pressing to investigate than our home's ultimate purpose. No, all of us, me as much as any of you, are here," she pointed at the main bridge console, "because we simply can't be there." Now the captain pointed down at the deck, but everyone knew she meant the main part of the ship. Society.

"We are, all of us, outcasts of our own making," she said, "and we prefer exile to that feeling of unbelonging we all shared down there. Is it so hard to imagine," she went on, "that someone born so different from the rest of Society, someone whose very existence is reviled by some people who should call him family, might want to escape just as we have?"

Oki had just finished *The Taming of the Shrew* and was into the first chapter of *Eoin's Butterfly* when she noticed that there was more ambient noise than usual. She was off-watch, in her quarters, but the door to the corridor wasn't soundproof and she could hear what sounded like the entire crew in the hall. She knitted her brow, marked her place in the text and put down her handheld. Ah, yes. The new crew member. That was today.

She left her quarters and followed the sound to the lock. The last time she had been here was when Evie arrived. How long ago had that been? Oki wasn't sure. She didn't understand other people's fascination with the passage of time. Each day was fundamentally the same as the day before and the day to come, and so it would be until she was too old to do her work. It was no different for the others, yet they seemed compelled to count each day as if the number were some sacred symbol.

The rest of the crew were already waiting by the lock when Oki arrived. "I was wondering if we'd have to come and get you," Ana said, her face tight. "We have to treat this as is it were a normal crew addition."

Captain Selani turned to face the mate. "Ana," she said. "It is normal. We need crew, we're getting crew. There's nothing unusual here."

"Nothing unusual?" Naomi interrupted. "Captain, you can pretend that this is just another day if you want to but that won't change the reality. Not only is a crew addition one of the most disruptive things that ever happens here, but to be getting a... to be getting... *him*. It's about as normal as being hit by an asteroid."

The captain opened her mouth, but whether it was to argue, explain or rebuke would remain unknown because the deep, sonorous tone of the lock sounded. All six women took a step back from the door, and even Oki noticed that she was holding her breath and her heart was beating faster than usual. Naomi was right, this was among the most exciting things that happened on the bridge—and anything exciting was also terrifying. As the lock began to cycle, Oki briefly had the incongruous thought to wonder what he would look like.

She wasn't sure who gasped, but someone did as the lock turned and a very ordinary-looking woman in a uniform stood in the centre. "Is that..." someone said, but was cut off by the woman stepping forward to the edge of the lock.

"Greetings from the people of the *White Cloud*," she said. "I am Navindra Mala, chair of the Crew Committee. We are here to introduce your newest member—Matthew Peelu." She stood to one side and another lock behind her cycled open. This time, there were no gasps, although even Oki was stunned at the new crew member's appearance. She remembered transitioned men from her time in Society and had seen images of biological males in stories from old Earth. She knew the ways in which their bodies were different, had read about how their hormones and upbringings made them unlike women. But that hadn't prepared her for—him.

He looked utterly ordinary and so terribly afraid.

"Welcome to the crew," the captain said, and Oki thought she could hear something odd in the older woman's voice. "We'll get you settled in your quarters, then you and I will have a private conversation. There aren't many of us, but we are in each other's pockets a bit up here and it can feel a little overwhelming at first. I remember my first day all those years ago—it was terrifying." She turned to face the women on the bridge. "Now give Matthew a little space, will you? There will be plenty of time for meeting and greeting later." They each took a step or two back, but none of them tore their eyes from the new addition. Oki remembered that it had been the same when Evie arrived and she remembered her own first day. She had been as terrified as Matthew now looked.

"Hello," he said, his hands visibly trembling. "I'm looking forward to working with you."

Navindra, the Crew Committee chair, stepped forward again. Oki had forgotten all about her. "We are confident that Matthew will be a fine addition to the crew, and we want to take this opportunity to thank each of you for your selfless commitment to this ship and its mission. Without," she turned pointedly at Matthew, who was nearly hiding behind the captain, "people like you, who are willing to give up family and community, we would never get anywhere."

The captain mumbled the appropriate reply and then the lock cycled shut. Oki caught the new crew member's eye and tried to identify what she saw there. Fear? Relief? Something unidentifiably masculine? She didn't know, but for the first time in as long as she could remember, she was intrigued by another human who lived outside the text of a story.

Oki waited an hour then went to the galley with her tablet. She'd read several chapters when she felt rather than saw a shadow in the doorway. She looked up, but it was only Jenn.

"Anything new in here from the Committee?" she asked, opening the hatch to the food bin.

"I don't know," Oki said, "I haven't looked."

Jenn stopped her rummaging and turned to Oki. "If you aren't here for food, then why are you here?"

Oki wasn't sure how to answer that question. She knew the answer, of course—she was hoping to talk to Matthew. But for reasons she couldn't articulate to herself, she didn't want to tell Jenn. She felt, for the first time in a long time since she had become a part of the Crew, uncomfortable with another person.

She stood and said, "I'll go."

"No," Jenn said, "you don't have to. I—" She turned away from Oki and leaned against the food storage unit. "I'm not really hungry, either. I guess I'm curious."

Oki sat back down and stared at her hands. Then, she picked up her tablet and continued to read. After a moment, Jenn sat down and picked up her tablet as well. They waited for hours. By the time he arrived in the galley, Evie had joined them as well. The look on his face when he saw half the crew in the small room made Oki feel guilty.

She stood and walked to the storage unit. "Are you hungry?" she asked. "The Committee provides fresh food—it appears here. We don't get a lot of choice but it is always good quality." She opened the unit and looked inside. "There is bread and cheese and some vegetables."

"Thank you," Matthew said, his voice quivering. He still had not stepped over the threshold into the room. "Um, do you usually eat meals together in... in here? The Committee told me..."

"No," Jenn said. "This is unusual. We were..." she looked around and caught Oki's eye. "We were curious. I'm sorry." She took a step toward the door and Matthew seemed to jump back to let her pass. Evie stood then as well, and slipped out the door.

"Maybe we can talk at watch change," she said without looking at him, and turned away to walk down the hall.

Oki held a loaf of bread and a hunk of cheese. She wondered if he would wait for her to leave as well, but he took a step toward her. "I don't do well in groups," he said, taking the food from her and keeping a good distance.

"None of us do," Oki said. "It's not usually like this. New people make us... different."

He nodded and turned to the counter. He started opening drawers and cupboards, and Oki let him find his way around. He made a sandwich and then sat at the small table. "I'll leave if you want," Oki said.

"It's okay," Matthew said. "I knew this wouldn't be easy, and the sooner I get used to you all the better it will be." He took a bite and Oki watched him chew. When he'd swallowed, he said, "You're the engineer?"

Oki nodded. "I was a mechanic in Society first—I worked in the engine room. I like machines, they are easy to understand. You just have to listen to them, you can hear where they are badly aligned or grinding. Not like people."

"When did you become Crew?"

Oki shrugged. "When I refused to have a baby. I'd been sent to the medclinic. They were preparing to admit me, when this woman in a nice suit arrived and talked to the doctors. I'd never even heard of Crew until then. I'd never thought about who ran the ship, made sure the course was true, kept watch. I just made sure the pumps pumped and the gears turned. But when she explained Crew life to me, I knew it was what I wanted."

"To run the ship?" he asked.

Oki shook her head. "To be left alone." She saw a look of recognition in his face, picked up her tablet and walked out the door of the galley.

"He's not like I thought he would be," Jenn said. Oki looked up from her tablet and waited for her to explain. "I mean, he looks so strange, but he's just like us." Oki said nothing and Jenn didn't elaborate. Eventually she gave an almost imperceptible shrug and turned away. Oki picked up her tablet again and Jenn left the bridge.

Oki didn't go back to her story, though. Something about what Jenn said bothered her. She didn't agree, but that wasn't uncommon. But she had a feeling in her stomach that reminded her of eating too much bread. Something about what Jenn said made her feel... uncomfortable.

She wondered what it would be like if someone said something like that about her. She knew she wasn't just like anyone else, even here in Crew. But it didn't bother her if people thought she was no different from them. What other people thought was usually not something that concerned her at all. No, it wasn't the comparison that bothered her. So it must be the comment about Matthew looking strange. Oki certainly didn't think he looked strange.

His skin was darker than her own, but he was paler than the captain. He was taller than Oki, but Evie was taller still. He kept his hair long, but so did she. He was slim, but Jenn could easily have fit into his clothes. He was, Oki thought, very average. She wondered what Jenn saw in him that was strange, and then wondered why that word seemed to bother her so much.

She checked the clock and saw that her watch was three-quarters done. The last few days, Matthew had taken to coming up to the bridge for the last hour of Oki's watch. He'd use the time together to ask her technical questions about the readouts and the ship's engine, but they didn't talk much. Sometimes he'd just stare out the port while she read. She found herself looking forward to the end of her watch and his company.

Right on time the door to the bridge slid open and Oki looked up to see Matthew come on deck. She nodded at him and he smiled, but neither spoke. He went over to his station and sat, poking at the screens. Oki put her tablet down and tried to remember how people began conversations about abstractions. None of the examples she could remember seemed appropriate.

"Why are you here?" she asked, after abandoning the various other openings she considered.

Matthew frowned. "Am I bothering you?"

Oki shook her head. "No, why are you here, in Crew? Why did you leave Society?"

"Oh," he said, and turned his chair to face her. He looked at her for a moment. "When was the first time you knew you weren't like other people?"

She thought. "I was in school," she said. "I liked school, more than the other children did. I didn't understand why they weren't more excited about learning things, but they didn't really have anything to do with me. As long as they didn't get in the way, I didn't care. But even then I thought it was something wrong with them—maybe that I was more mature, smarter... It wasn't until I overheard my teacher talking to my mother than I understood." Oki paused, remembering. She didn't like remembering this, but somehow she felt like it was important to tell it to Matthew. "My mother was crying, and I knew it was because of me. I think she thought that because I didn't cry and laugh like the other children that I didn't feel things, but I did. Seeing her cry because of me was hard. I..." She pursed her lips and thought about how she felt. "I think that was when I knew that there was something wrong with me."

Matthew nodded. "How old were you?"

"Six."

"Of course, I always knew," he said, "it was unavoidable. My first memory was trying to play with other kids in our sector and someone screaming for her mother to save her from the monster. All I'd done was ask to see her dolly." He shrugged. "My mother did her best, after all she had chosen to have me even once she knew I was going to be a boy. She knew it wouldn't be easy. But even when she put me in a playgroup with the other boys, it didn't get any better." He turned slightly to look out the port. He didn't say anything for a moment and Oki wondered if he was finished talking to her. Her tablet chirped, notifying her that she was now off-watch, but she made no move to leave the bridge.

"I don't know why it surprised her so much that I didn't fit in there, either," Matthew said, finally. "I guess she must have assumed that all my problems were about being a boy, but as soon as I met another boy I knew that wasn't it. It's just me, I guess." He turned to look at Oki. "Like you. We're not... typical."

"No," Oki said. "We're not."

It only took a couple of weeks before Matthew stopped asking Oki about technical details. He was quick and understood mechanics easily. She was pleased and thought he would make a good captain one day. He still joined her on the bridge at the end of her shifts, but they rarely spoke. She read and he puttered about, doing whatever it was that the ship's mate did. It was a fine routine until Evie began to join them.

She had no reason to be on the bridge, Oki thought. She was the purser, in charge of provisioning for their food and quarters. Oki tried to remember the number of times she'd ever seen Evie on the bridge outside of a crew meeting, and couldn't come up with any examples. Until Matthew Peelu had arrived. Now, she was finding excuses to be on deck almost every day. Every time she arrived when there was no reason for her to be there, Oki developed an itchy feeling all over her body. It wouldn't go away until either she or Evie left the bridge.

"So, are you getting acclimatized?" Evie asked Matthew, leaning against the bulkhead so that he couldn't avoid looking at her.

"Everything is fine," he answered. "I am sure I will be ready to take over for Ana when the captain moves on."

"Oh, I'm not worried," Evie said, leaning forward and putting her hand on his shoulder. Oki was trying and failing to ignore them, and caught Matthew's eye. She thought he looked itchy, too. She saw Evie lean in toward Matthew and whisper something. His eyes grew large and he stared at Oki. She could see him pushing his back into his seat, and wondered if he even knew he was doing it.

She coughed and put down her tablet with a clatter. Evie stepped back, and looked at her, her face scrunched into a frown. Oki looked back at her. "You don't belong here."

Evie's nostrils flared. "You laying claim to him, is that it?"

Oki didn't understand what she was talking about, but it didn't matter. "If you don't have work on the bridge, you shouldn't be here," she said.

"You can't watch him all the time," Evie said, narrowing her eyes at Oki, then walked off the deck.

"Thanks," Matthew said when she was gone.

"I don't like it when she's here," Oki said, "she doesn't belong."

Matthew nodded and turned back to his screen. Oki picked up

her tablet and read until her watch was over.

"Everything was fine until *he* got here," Naomi said. Evie was sitting in a corner of the galley, red in the face, while Naomi talked to the captain. Loudly. Oki stood just outside the door to the galley, not wanting to enter while the three women were in there. She hoped they would finish their conversation and leave soon; it was the time she usually ate.

"Naomi, Evie's behaviour has been inappropriate and just plain disturbing," the captain said, her voice lower but still easily heard from the hall. "For pity's sake, Ev, you're old enough to be his mother."

"But I'm not his mother," Evie said, her voice shaking.

"I can't believe the Committee didn't realize this would happen," Naomi said. "We can't be expected to just pretend he's one of us."

"It's not my fault," Evie said. "It's too much temptation."

"Well, either you get a hold of yourself," the captain said, "or we'll have to replace you."

"But he's the problem," Naomi said. "He should be the one who's replaced."

"Naomi," the captain said, sighing, "you do realize that he may be the only man in the crew today, but it won't stay that way. We are all going to have to learn to live together."

"I said it was a bad idea to start having boy children," Naomi said, "I knew it would cause problems."

"Maybe you were right," the captain said, "but it's done now and we just have to live with it. Now I don't want to see either of you until tomorrow at the earliest. I'm tired of this whole affair." Oki had to step back as Naomi and Evie left the galley. Evie wouldn't meet Oki's eyes.

She walked into the galley, where the captain was sitting at the table, her head in her hands. Oki went to the food unit and began making herself a meal. "Sometimes I wonder if we're all just wasting our time," she said. Oki didn't answer. "Do we really need to be filling the universe with more of our insecurities, our inability to recognize ourselves in each other? Are we really worth saving?"

"Are you asking me?"

"Sure," the captain said, a rare smile on her face. "Why not?"

Oki sat and thought. "I don't think we have enough information to know the answer," she said after a moment. "So we need to err on the side of survival. It is our nature, after all."

The captain nodded. "You're right," she said. "It is our nature, and that's both the solution and the problem."

Log Addendum, January 24, 2573, Crew Committee

This is the unabridged log of Captain Mathilde Hana. While the Committee has access to the log and does review its contents from time to time, it does not alter entries. Please be aware that the significant breaks between entries do not indicate removal of data. Captain Hana chose not to update the log with any regularity, and to discontinue her entries four decades before her captaincy ended. We regret the loss of her insights into that period.

Captain's Log—October 9, 2486

This feels ridiculous. I've been told that I have to start keeping a record, for the next captain. I don't know why, the automated ship's log will tell her everything she needs to know. But I couldn't think up a reason not to do it other than that I didn't want to, so here I am. Talking to myself.

So. New captain. I guess this is really for your benefit; maybe I should just address this to you, then. I'd feel a little less silly talking to someone specific, even if I don't know you.

You probably aren't even born yet.

I'm only thirty-one. I became Ship's Mate when I was nineteen, expected to be the Mate for a long time. That's how it usually goes. But Cheryl—Captain Sommer—she had that accident and I guess you could call it a battlefield promotion. Hopefully it won't go that way for you and me.

Funny, that. If nothing happens to me, when you hear this you'll be older than I am now. Now this feels even more ridiculous.

I can't do this.

End log.

Captain's Log, December 19, 2488

Hello again. It's been a while. Maybe you're even alive by now.

Whoever thought of something as maddening and annoying as Crew Committee should be locked away and doped. I mean, am I in command or am I not? Captain means in command. We're all educated up here, they know that. Hell, that's part of the requirements. Do they think we don't know what it means to captain a ship? Do they really think we aren't going to take this seriously?

Anyway, I've been told that I have to continue this idiotic log or I'll be replaced. As if this is the most important thing I could be doing. So I guess that's lesson number one for you: captain means responsibility without authority. And lesson two is keep a log. Getting the remains of humanity to new Earth, well, I guess that's just something that happens in between the log entries.

Committees. If I really were in command I'd disband the lot.

Captain's Log, June 27, 2489

You know how most days are spent just sitting around, drinking tea, looking at the screens and saying, "Yes. Everything is the same as it was yesterday and the day before and the year before and the decade before and so on..."? Some days aren't like that.

Space is mostly empty. We all know that. Look out the port and it's terrifyingly clear that, statistically speaking, there is nothing out there. Personally, I find it comforting, but if the rest of the crew are anything to go by, most people really don't like to think about it. However. Statistically speaking, in an infinite universe, nothing equates to something. And something hit us today.

It wasn't large, obviously, or we'd all be dead. And, Lani would have seen it on the longrange and we'd actually have had to steer this thing. But it was too small for that and by the time it showed up on the screens it was too late. Ping.

I remember learning about velocity and the strength of the hull and all the design that went into the ship. I knew we should be fine, and we were, and getting hit by a piece of dust really shouldn't be so terrifying. And yet. My hands are still shaking.

The worst part was there was nothing to do. It was going to hit us or it wasn't. It was going to be a problem or it wasn't. All we could do was wait and then react. Horrible.

After it was over, I sent one of the remote cameras out to inspect the damage. The report was clean, thankfully. No one has had to go out on my watch and I didn't want this to be the time. Honestly, I don't want it to happen at all. I may find the concept of the void comforting, but that doesn't mean I want to go out there into the heart of the thing. Or, worse, send someone else.

So. I suppose this is the kind of thing you have to look forward to. Not that it happens all the time—I hope this isn't going to happen again. But someday something will happen, something you can't do anything about, but you'll feel responsible because it's your job to be responsible.

Piss.

Captain's Log, April 25, 2490

I feel a bit bad about that last log entry. Makes it seem like I'm one of those moaners who hates their job but instead of doing something about it just complains all the time. So, let me tell you about today.

They restocked our provisions overnight so there was a fresh supply of fruit tea. I made a cup and went up to the bridge. It was the tail end of mid-watch and June was there. She likes to keep to herself so I just went over to the port and... oh, wasn't space beautiful this morning. Dark and deep and rich like you could just throw yourself into it. There were distant stars poking around the edges and I think I stopped breathing from the sheer wonder of it all.

And no one interrupted me.

And no alarms sounded or decisions begged to be made, I just got to have the moment.

We never talk about those moments. I think everyone is a bit embarrassed about it, really. We like to pretend we're all hard cases, shipped off to Crew because we were too tough for the rest of the ship. But it was too beautiful to keep to myself.

I can't wait for you to have a day like that.

Captain's Log, September 12, 2490

I had the strangest conversation with Karina. I wasn't sure if something was wrong—we aren't exactly close, but she seemed, I don't know, distracted? I'm not sure how long something has felt odd, but a few days ago I noticed it strongly. She was at her post, reading over the Committee's recommendations for new crew. I was reading over her shoulder; it's a bad habit, but I'm too too set in my ways to stop it now. Besides everyone is used to it, I reckon. Anyway, she was reading one of the applications, and I caught a few lines and must have make some kind of noise or something.

"What?" she asked turning to face me. She had a strange look in her eyes.

"That poor woman," I'd said. "Three sisters, can you imagine? No wonder she wants to get away from it all."

"I might have liked a sister," she'd said, then just put down her handheld and walked away.

At the time I hadn't figured it was anything important. We can all be a little short with each other, it's nothing. But then this morning it got even stranger. I'd just gotten up to the bridge, and found her staring out the port. This was strange enough—I can't ever remember a time when Karina got in before me. Still, I said hi or something and she whipped around and ran over to me as if she were starving and I was lunch. She grabbed my arm. I had to stop myself from tearing myself away.

"Mat," she said, her face way too close to mine. "Am I glad to see you."

"Okay. Everything all right?"

"No. Yes. Ugh, I don't know."

I got myself loose and walked over to the screens. The course was fine, nothing on the longrange that I could see. Lani wasn't in yet, but I understand the readout well enough. "Karina?"

"This ship is fine," she said, then collapsed into her chair. "It's me that's all wrong."

"Oh." I didn't know what to say. "You need meds?"

"No," Karina said, sounding miserable. "It's not like that. It's…" She stood up and walked back to the port. I could see a greasy spot where she's been leaning against it. "It's hard to explain. I think maybe I've changed, or maybe I just never really understood. I— I think I made a mistake, that's all."

"Anything I can help with?" I had no idea what she was talking about, but I had to say something.

"No," she said. And then she walked off the bridge.

I hope I'm not going to have to replace her. Breaking in new crew is no fun.

Captain's Log, December 3, 2490

Not everyone is crew material. This is something we all know— there's a reason why there's only a half dozen of us at time. But the whole point of the Committee is making sure that those of us who are selected are the right kind of people for the job. Not just that we understand the work, not just that we're competent, but that we're *suitable*. Cheryl once said that she wondered if the real reason there's Crew at all isn't to take care of the ship, but to take care of those of us who don't really fit into Society.

I think she was kidding.

Captain's Log, March 20, 2491

Karina told me today that she wants to go back to Society. I told her to think about it, give it a bit more time. I didn't know what else to say. I hope that she gets over whatever is causing this. I'm not sure that it's even possible to go back.

Captain's Log, April 5, 2491

If I had wanted to mollycoddle people having some kind of break-down, would I have spent my time in school learning about machines? Would I have ended up in Crew?

Lani woke me, saying I had to get to the bridge right away. When I got there I found her curled into a ball, crying. Karina.

"How can you live like this?" she said between sobs.

"Like what?"

"Alone, in this cage?"

"Do you mean the ship?"

She shook her head, but said, "Maybe."

I sat in my usual chair and waited. Either she would start making sense soon or she wouldn't, and I was awake already. Might as well see what this was all about.

"I told you," she said, finally. "I made a mistake."

"Moving to Crew."

"Yeah."

"The Committee explained that it was a permanent move."

"But I didn't know then," she said and the tears started fresh. "I mean, I knew it was permanent, but I didn't know how lonely I would be. How I'd miss my family."

"You hated your family," Lani said. I hadn't realized she was still there, but where would she have gone?

"Did you two know each other before you were crew?" I asked. Lani nodded.

"Not well, but we were from the same habitation sector." Lani turned back to Karina. "And you couldn't wait to get away from all of them. Same as me."

Karina shook her head. "I didn't know."

"Well," I said, "what you did or didn't know doesn't matter much at this point. What we have to decide is what's going to happen now." She just looked at me, this desperate expression on her face. "I'll contact the Committee," I said, "but you need to prepare yourself for the likelihood that you're not getting out of here."

I could see her visibly trying not to break down again, but she kept it together. "Thanks for trying, Captain." I nodded, but it wasn't as if I had a choice.

Captain's Log, May 6, 2491

I went to bat for her, I really did. I don't particularly want a crew member who doesn't want to be here, but I knew it was unlikely. Committee is pretty clear in the recruitment stage that this is a one way trip. That's all we do on this ship—one way trips. I read once where there used to be a saying, that it was a woman's prerogative to change her mind. I wonder whatever happened to that.

They said no.

It was a long and boring message, full of regulations and security, and I knew Karina wouldn't believe any of it. I certainly didn't. But the Committee is on the other side of the door and we're in here and they have the key. So we're stuck with each other.

The Committee sent another message, to my attention only. It was much less long and far more interesting. It was instructions to fabricate some medication that would help Karina "readjust"—whatever that meant. It sounded a bit sinister to me, but what could I do? We *are* stuck with each other. The crew decks are comfortable enough, but there's nowhere to go. Of course, that's the appeal to those of us who are suitable. The solitude. The silence.

But I guess it can be too much for some people. Makes sense, I suppose. I can't get enough of the view out the port, but I wouldn't want to have to go out there. Maybe it's the same for Karina. Maybe it turned out that she only liked the view.

So. Am I happy about drugging my navigator? No, I am not happy. Did I fab the stuff anyway, put it in her cup and pour the strongest tea I could brew in the hopes she wouldn't notice? What do you think?

Captain's Log, January 18, 2492

We aren't like Society people, with their individual lives, their families, their hopes and dreams. It's different, being Crew. Harder, sometimes. Simpler, sometimes. Better? Yes, I think so, but then that's why I'm Crew, why I'm Captain. If I thought I could live like them, like the breeding cattle they fundamentally are, then that's what I'd be doing.

So here it is, the big secret to the captaincy of the *White Cloud*: a computer could probably do the job. You must know it by now yourself—we are just a fail-safe, a backup to the automatic systems. When I became Crew, I thought I was making a real difference to the mission, to this ship. Most days, though, I am entirely unnecessary.

But here's the bigger secret, the secret of the whole mission: there might not be much to do on the bridge, but what there is *matters*. And I know I'd rather be doing something useful one day out of a thousand than just marking time every day of my life. In Society, the best anyone can hope for is that some of their DNA manages to survive in some long future descendant. This ship is just a giant seed pod.

At least you and I get a chance to steer.

Sheelagh was stuck. She knew it as clearly as she knew the sequence to open the door between the habitation sectors and the technical centre. She was stuck in a rut. Such a funny phrase to still be using, she thought. She'd seen seen images of ancient wheeled vehicles becoming mired in mud or snow, but there was really was no similar analogue here. There was sometimes mud in the arboretum or garden areas, but there were no vehicles large or weighty enough to really become stuck, and no traffic heavy enough to create ruts.

She sighed. "I'm doing it again," she thought. Wasting time pondering useless tidbits of information, obsessing over nuances of language. Getting lost in her own head. It was just one more of those things, the little routines, that defined her. They said that admitting you had a problem was the first step toward solving it, but that was not much comfort to Sheelagh. Simply knowing what was wrong was nowhere near the same thing as having a solution.

She pulled up the files on her tablet once more. She'd read them over three times already, but she would read them once more. Four times, that was the number. Any fewer and she felt uncomfortable and ill-prepared; more just seemed silly. It was an important decision. Few people were required to keep the ship running, but they were required. And someone had to pore through their education and work histories, their psychological assessments and expressions of interest. Sheelagh knew she was good at her job.

She had to choose one person to join the crew, a new stellar cartographer. It sounded dull to Sheelagh, but there were over a dozen candidates. She was shocked at the number of people excited by mapping stars. She had already eliminated all but three of the applicants, but she read through all the files anyway. At least, she skimmed them – that was good enough.

A knock sounded and she frowned. She didn't like to be disturbed when she was working. Actually, she thought, she didn't like to be disturbed at all. No one did, it was inherent in the connotation of the word. Interrupted, that was neutral, but disturbed was... well, it was disturbing. She forced herself to stop thinking about it and turned toward the open door.

"Yes?"

Liisa's familiar face poked around the doorframe. Her dark skin contrasted sharply with the pale walls of Sheelah's office. "Want to get some lunch?"

Sheelagh frowned. It wasn't midday yet. "You're early," she said.

"I know," Liisa answered, crossing the threshold and leaning up against the inside of the doorway. "There's some debris on the longrange, and I need to be back on the bridge before 1300. I figured a few minutes early wouldn't kill you."

"Of course not," Sheelah said, a tightness growing in her chest. "Let's go." She powered off her tablet, engaging the security program which would make her files inaccessible without her passcode. She slid the tablet into her pocket and stood.

Liisa arched an eyebrow, but didn't say anything about Sheelagh's somewhat redundant actions. They had been having lunch together weekly for nearly half a year—she knew that Liisa was accustomed to Sheelagh's rituals. As they walked down the corridor to the nearest galley, Liisa talked about the debris they had seen on the scanners and how the crew was planning to make minor adjustments in their trajectory to avoid the cluster. Sheelagh found the monologue tiresome, but said nothing. She counted her steps, pleased that the walk took the standard 472 strides.

She waited her turn at the galley, then made a simple salad and took a slice of fresh-baked bread. They sat at her second-choice table, the first choice taken by two people from the farming cooperative. Sheelagh began to eat: spearing first lettuce, then cucumber then tomato. She always counted when she made her salads so there wouldn't be a leftover piece of anything. Liisa was still talking.

"... the hull, but if one of the shards gets into the thrusters, or worse yet, scratches a sail, we'll all be completely boned. Not now, of course, but a few hundred years down the way. Just think about it —a nick today could fundamentally destroy our ability to maneuver on the deceleration leg." She shook her head and took a bite of her noodles. "It's kind of terrifying," she said after swallowing.

"Mhmm," Sheelagh said and noticed that the people at her first choice table had stopped their own conversation and were staring at them. She tried to remember if she knew their names, but nothing was coming. "Do you know them?" she asked Liisa, raising her eyebrows in the direction of the other diners. Liisa turned around, staring right at them, then turned back.

"Nope." She wound up another forkful of noodles and stuffed them in her mouth.

"Excuse me," one of the farmers said, "we couldn't help but overhear you talking. Are we..." she scooted her chair a bit closer to their table, "are we in any danger?"

Liisa finished chewing, then said, "Nothing more than usual. I mean, space travel is an inherently dangerous business. Appearances aside," she gestured at the comfortably-appointed galley, "there's only plastic and metal between all this and the murderous void. Not to mention that we're essentially a ballistic missile hurtling through space and time at a speed which would make our ancestors believe in gods." She shrugged. "So, yeah, we're in danger, but it's nothing exceptional." She turned back to her lunch, and grinned at Sheelagh. The faces of the farmers, though, were not smiling in the least.

Sheelagh was finalizing the transfer information for the new cartographer she'd chosen when her communicator began to flash. It was a very annoying red light that strobed not quite two times per second. The off-timing was worse than the colour. She put her tablet down and answered the call.

"We have a problem." Rhea's voice was tight and the lack of her customary greeting further indicated to Sheelagh that this was an urgent situation indeed.

"What can I do?" she asked.

"You can get your buddies on the bridge deck to stop scaring the pants off the regular folks on this ship," the head of technical staffing said. "I've spent the last two days averting a wide-scale panic. People seem to think that any second now some space rock is going to come hurtling through the hull and we're all going to perish in a fireball of death. It's ludicrous."

Sheelah frowned. "As far as I know, no one from the crew has ever said anything of the sort."

Rhea sighed. "I'm sure they haven't, but what they say and what people hear are two different things. The crew are trained professionals, whose main concern is making sure that we keep safely on course. Their concerns are more, shall we say, detail-oriented than those of the rest of us. And what they think of as the normal operating situation, someone with little knowledge of the realities of space travel will find terrifying. And that's exactly what's going on."

"I think I understand," Sheelagh said.

"Good. Now, as the liaison between the general population and the crew, could you please instruct them to be a bit more circumspect with what they say when they are off the bridge and among the rest of us? Please?"

"I will."

"Thank you. Now, I need to get back. This situation is far from resolved, I'm afraid." Rhea broke the connection, and Sheelagh found herself being glad not to have the other woman's job.

"Why won't you tell us what's really going on?" The woman was standing far too close to Sheelagh, and she was blocking the entrance to the office. Sheelagh blinked several times, her eyes and mouth suddenly dry. She had a sense of not being able to get quite enough air. The woman took a step closer and Sheelagh found herself pushing back into her desk. It was painful but she couldn't seem to stop herself. "What are you hiding?"

"I—" Sheelagh found it hard to speak. "N... Nothing."

"I don't believe you." The other woman's face was pursed into a scowl and she was close enough that Sheelagh could see her own face reflected in the woman's eyes. "There's something terrible happening, but we aren't being told. That's the only explanation for why no one on the crew will talk to us any more. Why they won't say anything about the ship. Well, we aren't going to stand for it. We have a right to know what's going on." Her whole body was trembling and Sheelagh wondered if she was going to become violent. She imagined how she might defend herself or hide, maybe use her desk as a shield. She was planning how she could dive under her desk, maybe get the chair between them, when the woman stepped back and shook her finger at Sheelagh. "This isn't over." Then she left.

It took Sheelagh several minutes before she was able to move from the position she'd backed into, and then she found that she was shaking too much to be able to work the communicator. She managed to get to the door of her office and shut it, even though she always felt uncomfortable in the small space when the door was closed. At that moment, discomfort was preferable to terror. She slowly lowered herself to the floor, back to the door, and curled into a ball. She waited patiently for the fear to pass.

"I don't know what to do about this," Rhea said. Her face was lined and there were dark circles under her eyes. Sheelagh thought that she appeared to have aged a decade in the past month. It was, she assumed, the burden of responsibility. Though she looked over at Jules and couldn't see that that the captain looked any different. People reacted differently to stress, she thought, and of course this problem was much more in Rhea's area of responsibility anyway.

"Sheelagh," Rhea's voice brought her out of her thoughts and back to the meeting. "Any ideas?"

She fought back the impulse to say that yes, of course, she had many ideas. Didn't everyone? They just weren't particularly applicable to this exact situation. Instead, she frowned. "This is what's called a no-win scenario," she said. "When the crew share technical information, most people don't have the relevant expertise to understand it. They misinterpret, and their ignorance breeds fear. But it's no better when the flow of information is terminated. People assume the worst, and because the crew are forbidden to talk about anything, there's no way to alleviate their fears. It seems to be an untenable situation."

Rhea's face dropped into her hands and she audibly sighed.

"If I might," the captain said. "I think I might have a solution. It might make things worse in the short term, but I believe it will forestall this problem in the long term. And as much as I realize that it will make your life much more difficult, we do have to think about the centuries to come."

"I'm listening," Rhea said.

Sheelagh knew that it was worse for Rhea and the other leaders. Rhea and her team had done their best to insulate Sheelagh from the worst of it, and she was grateful. But more than half the crew had resigned their positions in the wake of the new policy and Sheelagh's painstakingly assembled criteria had to be completely rethought. She also noticed that the number of applicants had drastically reduced. It puzzled her. For the first time, she found a role on the crew to be personally appealing.

Separating the crew from the rest of society was, she admitted, a drastic act. But the captain was right—over time, most people would be able to live their lives without ever really thinking about the reality of their precarious state. By separating the function of the ship from the function of society, both should be able to focus more on their own needs. It was a clever—if inelegant—solution.

But what a challenge finding replacements was proving to be. Liisa had resigned, as had the cartographer that Sheelagh had just chosen. It was not the situation she was accustomed to finding herself in. She reviewed the few applications once more—it was well past four times by now. As usual, the issue was not in the candidates' abilities. The Academy produced plenty of scientists and engineers, and Sheelagh had learned over the years that most of the crew positions could easily be picked up on the job by any well-educated person. The problem had always been personal suitability—and that was now even more difficult to address. If only more people were like her, Sheelagh thought, then this wouldn't be an issue.

She knew she was contemplating it long before she really began to accept that it was a real possibility. Sheelagh did not embrace change well—she had worked on crew selection her whole adult life, the idea that something else might be more fulfilling had always been irrelevant. This was what she did and that was all there was to it. But the idea that she could be segregated in a small area of the ship, with only a few other people she would ever need to deal with... the sheer predictability of that kind of life filled her with longing. It was her idea of paradise.

As for the work, it would be fine, she knew. She'd had to become reasonably conversant with all the crew positions, and she felt that she could probably be competent at some of them. Stellar cartography was most likely the best choice. Maybe she would even come to find the idea of mapping the stars exciting. Though it wasn't excitement she wanted. It was routine. A lack of interruptions. Schedule. Predictability. Solitude.

She told herself that she hadn't made a decision, that she wasn't about to abandon everything she had ever known and lock herself behind a door. She told herself that it wasn't happening even as she packed her few belongings and steadfastly refused to find a suitable candidate for the stellar cartographer. But when Rhea called, demanding that she finalize the crew roster, she couldn't hide the truth from herself any longer.

"I believe I've found all the replacement crew members," she said. "But there is one opening I'm afraid that you will have to fill."

Takara longed for the wind. She had heard about it when she was child, but hadn't really understood what it meant until she saw it in a story from old Earth. It wasn't important to the plot, just a moody shot of a leaf blowing down the street, but it captivated Takara. To feel the air moving on her face, strong enough to carry a small animal away—it was all she dreamed of. She spent hours in the arboretum, where the tiniest breeze blew from the atmospheric processors located nearby, lying on her back with her eyes closed, waiting for the touch of the air on her skin. But it wasn't enough. It was never enough.

"Plenty of people don't love their work, Tak," Simone scowled at her friend over bowls of soup at the canteen. "That's why they call it 'work.' You've got to just pick something, or the council will choose for you and you really don't want that."

"Why not?" Takara said, only partly to bother Simone. She'd been Tak's closest friend since Simone and her mother had moved into the quarters three doors down, and their friendship had always been based on mutual annoyance as much as anything else.

Simone grunted then slurped her soup. The sound drove Tak crazy. "How do you think they get people to do the shitty jobs? If you can't make up your mind—poof! You're the new toilet unblocker."

Takara laughed. "They have machines for that."

"You sure?" Simone said, looking at Tak through the fringe of frizzy hair that covered her eyes.

Tak shrugged. "Maybe I'd like unblocking toilets. It's useful, I'm sure there's a real sense of accomplishment you get when you clear out a load of shit." She couldn't keep up the pretence any longer and started to laugh. She could see Simone trying not to join but it didn't take long before they were both laughing. An old lady a few tables over made a disgusted noise at them which only set them off even harder. Tak's stomach hurt by the time they managed to get themselves back under control.

"Seriously," Simone said, "you do need to think about this. There's got to be something that interests you, at least a little. You said you used to hang out in the arboretum—why not be a gardener or something?"

Tak shook her head. "I don't like the dirt."

"What about a botanist, then? Something in hydroponics?"

"You need Academy training for that." Both of them knew that Tak's school history wasn't going to get her in the Academy. The best she could ever hope to do was start some job at the bottom and work her way up internally.

"I'm trying to help you out here," Simone said, all traces of their laughing fit gone. "There are only a few days left before you need to put in your apprenticeship requests. If you don't come up with something on your own, I'm going to have to do something drastic."

"Like what?" Tak asked, rolling her eyes. "Tell my mom?"

"Nope," Simone said, a nasty grin forming on her face. "I'll sign you up for childcare."

Tak's eyes got large. "You wouldn't?"

Simone shrugged. "If you don't want to clean up shit one way or another, you'd better pick something." Before Tak could say anything more, Simone stood up and took her bowl to the cleaning station. She left the canteen without another word.

She wouldn't really do that, would she? Tak was terrible with kids. She didn't like them, they didn't like her. She hadn't even liked other children when she was one, it was one of the reasons she spent so much time by herself with the trees. Maybe Simone was right, maybe she should try to find something in gardening. Surely there was an entry-level job there that she could do.

She took her lunch dishes to the cleaner and headed back to her quarters, determined to choose something. Really, how hard could it be?

Tak's mother was home when she arrived. "Is everything okay?" Tak asked. Her mother was rarely home during work hours.

Candace shook her head. "They're rerouting the phase inducers or something." Tak thought her mother was oddly proud of her lack of understanding about the systems on which she worked. "Whatever it is, we can't take any of the filters out while it's happening, so we all got sent home. It's no holiday, though, because we'll all have to work doubles once the whatsits is done with." She rolled her eyes. "You'd think they could come up with a better system. I mean they have to do this every half year, and every time it's as if it's never happened before. Total panic."

"Sure," Tak said. She'd listened to her mother rant about the management of the sector where she worked more than a few times. It was the main reason Tak had vowed not to end up on the environmental team. Though she was starting to wonder how much of it was just her mother's personality. She had the feeling that it wouldn't matter where she was, what work she was doing, her mother would find something to complain about.

Tak knew that Candace was a fundamentally unhappy person and it was her own greatest fear that she would end up just like her mother. Like Tak, Candace had not excelled in her early education and hadn't been Academy material. Of course, that wasn't anything to be ashamed of—less than 10% of graduates went on to the Academy. But now that Tak was at the age to be entering the workforce it had become clear to her that there wasn't much available for a normal person. It was all scut work, cleaning up literal or figurative shit. And Tak knew from a lifetime of living with Candace that cleaning up shit just wasn't all that rewarding.

She went into her small room and shut the door. She pulled up the list of available entry-level positions in Blue Sector. There was nothing new on the list, and she'd already discarded all of them as boring at best or totally unsuitable at worst. She wondered how hard it would be to change sectors. People did it—Simone and her mother had come from Yellow. But Simone's mom was on the bridge crew, which was why they moved. Tak knew there was nothing special about her that would make a manager pick her over someone local. She scowled. There had to be more to life than this. But in all her eighteen years, she'd never quite figured out what that might be.

"Did you get the stuff?"

"Yeah," Simone's friend Emil whispered, even though there was no one anywhere near them. Tak, Simone and Emil were well hidden in the hollow of a cedar bush in an out-of-the-way corner of the arboretum. And it was the middle of the night. No one was going to catch them. Emil pulled a large bottle of slightly murky liquid from a bag and held it up.

"Are you sure this stuff is safe?" Tak asked.

"Oh come on," Simone said, grabbing the bottle and twisting off its cap. "It's the same stuff they serve at that bar all the tradies go to. Angela next door is always coming back from there all drunk and stupid. It's fine." She fixed Tak with a stare that was equal parts derision and self-justification. She slugged back a healthy amount and managed not to cough or sputter. "See," she wheezed. "Fine."

Tak laughed but took the bottle. She took a tentative swig and was surprised at how not completely horrible it was. "I think this is a sipping drink," she said, handing the bottle back to Emil.

They got through about half the bottle before they really slowed down. By then, the liquor was starting to take effect and Tak noticed that Emil was leaning on Simone, looking half asleep. She nudged the two of them and said, "We better do something or you're going to pass out."

"Any suggestions?" Emil asked.

Tak frowned. "Can I ask you a personal question?"

"Sure," Emil shrugged.

"How did you know that you were different from everyone else?" Emil had transitioned before Tak had met him.

"I never saw it that way," he said, pulling himself up to try and focus. "It wasn't that I was different from other people so much as I wasn't the person people saw when they looked at me. I never felt out of place or anything, but I just wasn't the little girl other people expected me to be." He shrugged again and reached out for the bottle. "It probably helped that one of my teachers was living as a man, so I didn't have to figure out what I was all on my own. I can't imagine how hard it must have been for the first person on the ship to decide that there was something wrong with his body."

"It's not like there's a shortage of things that are wrong around here," Tak said, taking the bottle from Emil.

"What do you mean?" he asked.

"I mean it's horrible being stuck on this ship, being forced to have babies, having so few options in life. On Earth people had the freedom to choose what their futures would be. Here... we're just slaves to some future world we'll never see."

"You're not thinking about how things really were on Earth," Emil said. "Pollution, poverty, war, disease. There's a reason we left, Tak."

"That's what they tell us," she countered. "We don't know that any of that is true."

"Sure," Simone said, "this is all just a big conspiracy to make us do boring jobs we hate, right?"

"Maybe it is. How would you know?" Tak said.

"Hey, you know what we should do?" Simone said, a gleam in her eye.

"What?"

"We should go and sneak onto the bridge! My mom took me once but they never showed me anything important. I bet we could get in there now and find out what's really going on. That would show them."

"Simone," Emil said, "I don't think we could sneak into the canteen in our current state. As it is, we're going to be lucky to get back to our quarters without getting caught." He shook his head. "Besides, what are we going to see on the bridge anyway? Stars? Some complicated console for flying this thing? Big deal. We're stuck here regardless of why they left in the first place. All we can do is make the best of it." He picked up the bottle, now getting close to empty. "To making the best of it." He took a swig and passed it over to Tak.

"Yeah," she said and drank.

"Okay, so our choices are limited. I get that. And yeah, it blows airlock that we're going to get stuck with boring jobs that no one would ever want to do. But there's more to life than your job."

"Are you really sure that's true?" Tak asked Simone, slowly licking the drug-laced fruity pop. Emil's connection was really good. "Really, who do we know that has anything interesting going on besides work? And having a family doesn't count."

Simone frowned while absently sucking on her own drugstick. It made her look like a sulky baby. "I mean," she said around the stick, "just because no one we know can be bothered to make something of their lives doesn't mean it has to be the same way for us. At least we know everything we do is pointless."

"Oh right, that's a big help." Tak sighed.

"Sure it is," Simone said. "You don't think that our moms thought that they would be doing work that a robot could do better? You don't think they thought that raising the next generation of space babies wasn't going to be the most fulfilling thing in the universe? Of course they bought all those lies, just like almost everyone we know buys them, too. It takes a special understanding of things to see past all that." Simone nodded thoughtfully and Tak had the momentary thought that if she'd been more interested in academics, Simone would have made a pretty good teacher. She had that self-important, smug look down pat.

"Right," Tak said, smirking. "You and me, we've got a monopoly on the truth. As if."

Simone frowned. "Still, I'm right about one thing at least: we don't have to be defined by our jobs. We can do other stuff, be who we want. That's the trick of it, though." She got in close to Tak's face and Tak was too high to think about moving out of the way. She wondered for a moment if Simone was going to kiss her, but then she just kept talking. "What *do* you want to do? If you had a choice, if this was old Earth. What would you do?"

Tak knew it was the drug but at that moment she felt like that question was the most important thing anyone had ever said to her. What did she want? Who was she, really?

She thought about it for what seemed like a long time. Finally, she said, "I don't know."

Simone nodded. "Exactly," she said, as if that answered some eternal debate. "Exactly." She pocketed her drugstick, punched Tak in the arm a little too hard, then walked away.

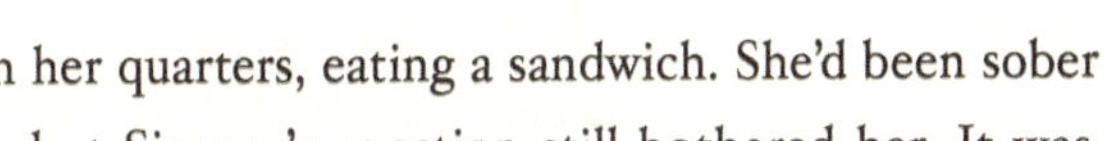

Tak sat in her quarters, eating a sandwich. She'd been sober for two days now, but Simone's question still bothered her. It was hard to think about what she wanted, when she'd spent her whole life with her options so limited. She tried to imagine herself as an old woman —what would she like to remember about her life? She couldn't come up with much.

The only moments she cared about now were getting high with Simone and Emil. It wasn't much of a life goal, but spending time with them was fun. She liked the way she felt when she didn't have to think so much, and she liked being with them. It was like a cool breeze on her skin. Even when they were mean, it was fun.

She didn't have an artistic inclination—she couldn't draw, didn't have the patience for music and reading. She liked watching stories, but didn't see herself as a filmmaker. It wasn't something she could make a living at anyway, even if it did appeal. As for any job she'd really be able to get... the last thing she imagined ancient Takara thinking fondly about was some menial grind day in day out.

And that left family, and she knew that wasn't it, either. She couldn't manage to make herself care about children or grand-children, it just wasn't in her. She knew that she was no intellectual genius, and so her only real value on this ship was as a step along the way—a link in the human chain from old Earth to new Earth. She wasn't so dumb that she didn't understand the importance of survival, she just couldn't bring herself to care about it personally. What difference could one person make, anyway?

Maybe she could spend her life just doing whatever job she got stuck with, then having a good time in her off hours. People had done that for centuries, if the stories she watched were accurate. Sure, she couldn't run off and have an adventure in Thailand or meet some amazing new person at a baseball game, but surely there was a way to enjoy herself here. Even if it just meant making sure that Emil never lost contact with his supplier.

She finished her sandwich and sat back in her chair. Was it so wrong to want some joy out of life? Why should people whose interests naturally aligned with the requirements of shipboard life get all the fun? It wasn't fair. "Life isn't fair," her mother always said, but why did it have to be that way? Wasn't it just another way of giving up? Tak wasn't ready to give up, not yet. Not when she was just about to have the most freedom she'd ever get.

Tak couldn't remember how long it had been since she had been to the arboretum during the day. It was strange to see other people there, strange to not be worried about making too much noise or disturbing the plants. It made her feel simultaneously like a real adult and like she was a kid again. She walked along the path, looking at the trees—they were so different from each other. The thin, fragile willows, the tough-barked elm. So many she couldn't even name. It was funny, for someone who spent so much time here, she knew very little about the trees. She climbed her way up the little hill, remembering how she used to run up this path when she was young. It had seemed like a mountain to her then, she used to pretend she was climbing to the top of a peak on Earth. Funny, she never specified which Earth...

As she walked up the hill now, it seemed like not much more than a slight rise in the dirt. She knew it didn't matter which Earth she thought of, the images in her mind had no bearing on any reality. They were an amalgam of stories passed down and distorted from generations on the ship, combined with images from stories she'd seen. And, of course, it would never matter how accurate her fantasies were. She would never see a planet with her own eyes, never step on terra firma in any star system. She was in between, homeless.

She got to the top of the hill and found her prize. A waft of breeze that came up from the grassy side of the hill. It was warm and humid, the arboretum's atmosphere adjusted to best suit the plants. She could smell the trees on the air, feel the wind on her face. She closed her eyes and images of a fabricated Earth filled her mind. She imagined the heat of a day star on her face, the tang of an ocean in the air. She imagined a life for herself that might have been, had she been born in another time, another place. She stood there, revelling in her fantasy, for minutes or hours.

Finally, she opened her eyes again. There was no change in the light, no external indication of how much time she had been there. She could check her tablet, but she didn't care. There was nothing she needed to do, nowhere she needed to be. She was, entirely, unnecessary.

She began to walk down the hill, and looked over the arboretum as she did. She could see the neat rows of trees, some bearing fruit, the shrubs and bushes with their berries and fragrant herbs. She saw people, too, some working with their hands in the soil, others walking the paths like she was, enjoying the plants and the scented air. It was life, in all its mediocrity and routine. Like the trees, which rooted wherever their seeds landed at the whim of the wind, so too were people at the mercy of their circumstance.

Tak filled her nostrils with the scent of the trees, and held the memory of a life she would never experience in her mind as she went back to her quarters to find something she could care about in this world.

"I cannot believe this actually worked." Linae stepped back from the console screen and shook her head. "This is... I don't know."

"I have never seen you literally speechless before," Sunni said, her arm around Linae's waist. "I'm so proud of you."

Linae took a deep breath, but the air caught in her throat. She had never been much of a weeper, but Sunni would have sworn the other woman was holding back tears. She and Sunni and the others had been working on this for so long, but Sunni knew that Linae had never allowed herself to truly believe it was possible. And yet, here it was—a functional simulation of a complete personality. It was utterly amazing.

"Hello," the face on the screen had an expression of curiosity and mild confusion. "Linae, Sunni, you look... strange. Am I— am I where I think I am?"

"Yes," Sunni said, looking into the camera mounted clumsily atop the screen unit. "We did it, Hélène. You're a copy of the real— I mean, the first Hélène's personality. How do you feel?"

The image on the screen appeared to freeze for a moment, then she smiled. "I feel fine. Normal, I guess. I can't feel my body, which is suppose makes perfect sense since I don't have one. But I didn't notice that until I started to really think about it. It's not like the absence is obvious—I don't feel sick or injured. Just... disembodied. It's oddly not odd, if you know what I mean."

Sunni laughed. "I do know what you mean. Is it," she looked at Linae, who seemed to have completely lost her ability to speak, "is it comfortable?" Her voice lowered and she squeezed Linae. "Is it horrible?"

"No," Hélène said and smiled. "I remember —" She broke off and appeared to look down. "Well, it feels like a memory, anyway. Look, I'm just going to talk as if my memories are really mine, it's just too confusing to try and get the language right."

"Of course," Sunni said.

"I remember us talking about whether this was immoral, if we were making a kind of prison. And there was no way to know without asking someone who was," she looked from side to side and it appeared eerily as if she were seeing the edges of the screen. "Who was in here. So I volunteered. And now, here I am."

"And…"

"And it's fine," she smiled again. "I know intellectually that I am not real, that when the device is powered down that I am, more or less, dead. But I also know that when Hélène's body dies, I will still be here. It's comforting, in a strange way."

"What is?"

"To exist out of time."

Sunni felt something break in Linae, some force she had been using to maintain her composure. She heard a sob and Linae broke down, the tears falling freely.

"Hey now," Hélène said, "it's okay, that's what I'm saying. Come on, Lin, I'm fine in here, really. We did it, we really did. We've changed everything."

Linae buried her head into Sunni's shoulder and wept. Sunni caught Hélène's eye and the image on the screen shared the real Hélène's look of concern mixed with amusement. "Oh, Lin," Hélène said, "you should really get some sleep.

Sunni took Linae back to their quarters, fed her and put her to bed. Hélène was right—Linae had been lead on this project and as they'd gotten closer to testing it, she had been spending all her time working on the final touches.

"I'm not tired," she'd protested once they gotten back to their room and Sunni had insisted she get some rest. "There's still so much to do. We have to document the trial, and there's a list of test questions we need to ask the Hélène construct, and..."

"And it will all still be there tomorrow," Sunni said. "For now, I'm not letting you out of here, so you might as well sleep. You won't be able to do anything else." Linae had begun to protest but Sunni put on her serious face and before she knew it, Linae had fallen asleep. Sunni kissed her lightly on the forehead and closed the door on her way back to the main room of their quarters.

Linae had always been intense about work. About everything, really, Sunni thought. One of the things she liked about being with Linae was that she got to be the laid-back one for a change. She had been a serious child by the standards of her family. Hers had been unusual in that there were three children and her sisters and parents were very much free spirits. Art, fun, food—they were the driving forces in their wild quarters. Sunni's studious and inquisitive nature wasn't stifled, but it was often gently mocked. Only once she'd become part of the bridge crew and met Linae had Sunni realized that she wasn't the most serious person on the ship.

Sunni stretched out on the couch and let it all sink in. It worked. It really worked. All those years of modelling, of listening to people tell them it was impossible. It was a little hard to believe.

She wondered what they would do now. She, Linae and Hélène had been working on this project in their spare time for years. There was a lot of down time on the bridge and everyone had their hobbies. Hélène, their welder and engineer, had joined them more recently but put in no less time or energy in the project.

In her less charitable moments, Sunni sometimes wondered if one of the reasons she and Linae had become a couple was neither of them had time for anyone else. Certainly, all the time they spent together had a lot to do with it. But she could no longer imagine her life without Linae. Ultimately, she thought, it didn't matter what brought people together, whether it was an unstoppable attraction against all odds or dull utility. She was grateful for Linae however they'd managed to get together.

She began to realize that she was starting to fall asleep on the couch. She pulled herself upright and took her own advice. She slipped into bed next to Linae and fell asleep wondering what it would really feel like to live as a mind in a box.

"This will certainly be remembered as one of the first great achievements for our society aboard the *White Cloud*," Hine Manti said, standing atop the small stage that had been erected in the engineering hall, "and it is remarkable that it will be the very tool used to convey our legacy to future generations. We are lucky to be able to bear witness to this moment, this unique time in human history."

Sunni nudged Linae. "She sure does like to talk," she whispered. Linae elbowed her and from her other side, Hélène snorted.

"Shhh," Linae said, and shifted from one foot to another. Sunni had never seen her so nervous. Linae had a tendency to keep her emotions and concerns to herself, to take on too much on her own. It was annoying at work and maddening at home. Maybe things would change now.

Hélène shot Sunni a look of mock exasperation as the head of the Academy droned on. The entire faculty and most of the students were in the audience, as well as many prominent members of the community. It was the largest assembly of people Sunni had ever seen on the ship, and she wondered if there had ever been this many people in one place on board before. It was exactly the kind of question that future generations would be able to answer by asking someone who was there. The thought that she had helped make that possible was intoxicating.

"So, in conclusion," Hine said, and Sunni was certain she could hear a collective sigh from the audience, "I'd like to thank the team who have worked tirelessly on this project for years. I give you Hélène Maarten, Sunni DeWitt and Linae Cook."

Applause filled the hall as the three walked up to the stage. Sunni felt her stomach lurch when she turned to see the crowd of people looking at them, at her. She squeezed Linae's hand.

"Thank you, Hine," Linae said, turning to the Dean. "We are all very proud and excited by the success of this project. Humanity has been trying to conquer death since the beginning of time. We have not done that, but we have given our descendants a connection with their past that until now has been at best an imperfect understanding of history. Now, our great-grandchildren will be able to truly interact with their ancestors, the emissaries of the past. We are humbled to have played a part in this development."

Linae turned to the construct station on display behind them. This proper prototype was a vastly improved version of the initial drive, screen and camera system that they had used for testing. She flipped a switch and the inlaid screen brightened. It felt like a hour passed to Sunni before the image of Hélène's construct filled the screen.

"What a wonderful turn out," she said and the audience went mad. Some gasped, others cheered and Sunni saw someone have to catch one elderly woman before she fell to the ground. "I am so pleased that you have all come to see me, and I am very happy to know that I and others like me will be able to visit with your descendants for centuries to come."

Spontaneous applause broke out, and the construct waited patiently for it to die out. "However," she went on, "there is one very important aspect to this project which has been ignored until now. I have discussed this with the three people with you now who have helped make this a reality, and we agreed that it was important to tell the whole story. You see, my corporeal doppelgänger and her teammates did not invent this process. They worked long and hard, yes, to make it work, but the genius behind this device lived three generations ago. Her name was Ella Mikkels, and she was not as lucky as we have been to have such a supportive scientific community."

There were murmurs of confusion among the crowd. Linea reached over and took Sunni's hand again. Hélène—the human Hélène—reached over and put her arm around Sunni. The three of them stood there as a unit, as the construct explained the terrible history of the invention.

"Ella did not manage to create a prototype of her invention, she never saw this process in reality. She could only imagine this moment, but she knew that it was possible. As you can see, she was right. However, the rest of her society did not share her vision. Ella was discredited, her work hidden for years. She, herself, was ultimately stripped of her duties and diagnosed as delusional. She was contained in a medical facility for the rest of her life.

"When Linae Cook came across Ella's work in an old file, she immediately believed that it was possible. She, along with Sunni and myself—that is, Hélène—devoted their lives to realizing Ella's dream. But it was Ella's dream, Ella's work that has made this a reality. And that is why we are asking that the record show that this is Ella Mikkels' creation."

"It's not their decision to make," Linea said, leaning over the table.

"I realize that," Hine said, a placating look on her face. "The council just wants you to reconsider. For a breakthrough like this to be, well, disavowed is—"

"No one is disavowing anything," Sunni said, her voice rising. "We are proud of our work. Do you think this was a decision we came to lightly? Do you really think we devoted our lives to create something revolutionary, and don't want to take the credit? Of course we'd like to be remembered for creating the Ghosts. But we didn't. It's Ella Mikkels' design, her creation. It should be her name in the records."

"If it hadn't been for the fear and cowardice of her peers," Hélène said, "she would have been the one to make the first machine."

Hine sighed. "Fine. I can make it work with the council. But they won't like it and frankly, I don't either." She looked at the three of them, her eyes boring into each of them individually. "You do see the irony, don't you? The very people who have made it possible to bring history to life, to truly keep the record accurate, are forcing me to falsify the historical record."

No one said anything for a moment. Then Linae spoke. "Sometimes the facts don't tell the whole truth."

Most days Sunni wondered if the compromise had been worth it. "I don't understand why we had to give up anything at all," she said, not for the first time.

"The council wants to forget all about Ella Mikkels," Linae said, "what was done to her. It's an embarrassment..."

"It's worse than that," Sunni said.

"Yes," Linae said, "it is. And that's exactly why they did not want us to give her the credit. It's awkward for them, very awkward."

"But to agree to go along with this ridiculous contest..." Sunni spit out the last word as if it were rotten. "It goes against everything we were trying to achieve with the Ghosts."

"And that's the consequence of our choice," Linae said. "When we gave up claim to the machines, we gave up our right to have any say about how they are used."

"But it's wrong," Sunni said. "The machines should be for the wisest, most knowledgable, most important of us. At least, some of them should be kept for people with knowledge we want to keep."

"I think so, you think so, Hélène thinks so," Linae took Sunni's hand, and she felt her heartbeat slow at Linae's touch. "But the council thinks that it's more fair to allow anyone to become a Ghost. And— I can see their point."

Sunni pulled her hand away and felt the heat rising in her chest again. "You see their point? Did we work so hard to make this technology so they could be filled with ordinary people who don't even understand the gift they've been given? There can only be so many Ghosts—they should be important people, useful people."

Linae smiled and waited for Sunni to stop pacing. "Everyone is important," she said, quietly.

"Sure," Sunni said, "but not everyone is timeless." She turned and walked out of their quarters.

"Have you seen this?" Sunni barged into Hélène's quarters, brandishing her tablet in the air. "I don't know whether to laugh or cry."

"The contest?"

"Yes, the *contest*." Sunni's face was a mask of disgust. "I never really believed they would do it. I always thought that someone would realize that this is an opportunity that we can't afford to waste. There are teachers in the Academy, artists... hell, even *Hine* would be a better choice than some random person chosen by lottery." She slumped on to the couch and let her head fall into her hands. "I wonder why we even bothered."

Hélène's face became cloudy. "I don't understand why they see it as a prize to be won," she said. "It's a duty, a burden. The price of being a part of history." Sunni thought she could see Hélène shiver. "It's almost ironic—Ella Mikkels being imprisoned for her creation which is, in many ways, a kind of prison itself."

"And that's another thing," Sunni said, "I can't believe they are altering the records to take out all the references to what happened to her. It's not just that she'll be credited with the invention—they're making it look like she actually built the prototype herself."

"Things have gotten away from us," Hélène said. "I wonder if we should have stuck to the bridge."

Sunni shook her head. "We were trying to do the right thing. I never thought that it would end up like this."

"We should do something."

"Like what?" Sunni asked. "Try to overthrow the council? No one is going to listen to a bunch of gearheads. Even the people who know what we've accomplished aren't going to support us against the whole council. Especially since we're the ones who asked for the record to be changed."

"There has to be something we can do." Hélène said. "Something to tell the future what really happened."

Sunni frowned, then smiled. "Of course there is," she said. "And we've already done it."

"So, you really think no one is going to notice an extra person in here?" The image of the Hélène construct looked remarkably like Hélène did when she was having a hard time accepting someone's ridiculous ideas.

"You'll only need to hide for a generation, two at the most," Sunni said. She was whispering, even though there was no one else in the room. Hélène was keeping watch outside and they'd decided not to even tell Linae. Sunni told herself that the fewer people who knew about this, the easier it would be to keep the secret, but she worried that Linae wouldn't approve.

Since the machine had gone online, Sunni had found herself drifting apart from Linae. Maybe it was the lack of a common focus, maybe it was Linae's blind acquiescence to the council's requirements. Regardless, Sunni had found herself spending more time with Hélène and now she didn't think she could possibly talk to

Linae about their plans. She hoped that once the new constructs were installed in the machine and the Hélène construct was safely hidden away, that things might go back to normal.

"When we gave the council the requirements for installing the new Ghosts," she said to the machine, "we gave them the net details—the schematics with you already in there. If you stay inaccessible for, say, a hundred years, there's no way they'll ever know you're there."

The image on the screen shook her head. "I hope you're right," she said. "Do you think they would erase me if they found me?"

Sunni shook her head, but said, "I don't think so. But really, I don't understand their thinking at all. Part of me worries that this is all about controlling information, making sure that the council can determine what version of history is passed on."

"People have always tried to control how they are remembered," Hélène said. "I'll do my best."

"That's all any of us can do," Sunni said. She smiled at the image of her friend one last time, then began to type the commands which would hide the construct program. She felt her stomach lurch as the screen winked out and the image of Hélène disappeared. She had to blink back tears as she finished.

"How did it go?" Hélène asked as Sunni crept out of the room.

"Okay," Sunni said and turned to her friend. "Do you think we did the right thing?"

"About what? Hiding the construct? Going along with the council?"

"No," Sunni said, "building the machine in the first place. There's something terrible about watching someone just turn off like that..." She saw a look pass over Hélène's face and reached out to touch her arm. "She's fine. She said so herself. She would have told us if it was... unpleasant."

Hélène didn't say anything for a moment, her eyes looking at something in the distance only she could see. "I'm sure you're right," she said.

Kris stared out the porthole, the deepness of space vast and empty before her. There was nothing to see, but she wan't really looking. It had been four days since the funeral ended. The long, interminable funeral.

The entire ship grieved for Moana, the last of the original crew. Moana Hue, the last hero of the *White Cloud*. Everyone aboard paid tribute to her, bemoaned the loss to their culture, declared how special she was to them all, but she was Kris's *mother*. Where was her private grief? Where was her moment to weep not for the end of an era, but for her personal loss?

Something caught her eye and she momentarily thought it was something outside the ship, but it was just a reflection in the port. She turned to see Captain Toov standing behind her. "How are you holding up?"

Kris shrugged. "Mum was old. We all knew it would happen sooner or later. But…"

The captain took a step toward her and put a hand on her shoulder. She squeezed lightly. "It don't think it matters how much we're prepared for it," the captain said, "it still hurts when they go." Kris nodded. "We can manage a few days without you, if you want to take some time."

"Thanks," Kris said, "but I think I need the distraction."

The captain nodded. "Well, if you change your mind, just say the word. I know you haven't really had a lot of time to take care of yourself."

"I'll be okay," Kris said and she believed it. With her mother being the last living original crew member, she had been the last of her peers to have her parent die. She knew that she would be fine, everyone else was fine. It was the way of life. Everything that lives will die. She knew all this. But somehow it didn't feel normal. It felt like the end of everything.

"How are you doing, mum?" Penny leaned against the doorjamb, her brows furrowed. Kris almost laughed—she had the concerned parent look down pat.

"Everyone keeps asking me that," Kris said. "Do I look like I'm about to have a breakdown or something?"

"No." Her daughter was so much like a mother hen, Kris sometimes wondered where she got her personality. She didn't know much about the sperm she'd used to get pregnant—all they did was make sure there wouldn't be some kind of genetic problem. Otherwise it was lucky dip. She guessed that the seed stock must have had a particularly nurturing temperament. "We're just concerned. It's a hard time for you right now."

Kris bit back a snarky reply. It was hard to remember that her daughter was an adult woman, soon to be a mother herself. She had opinions, ideas and knew probably at least as much about life as Kris did herself. It just felt wrong to be given advice by her own child. "Thanks for worrying about me," Kris said, "but I'll be all right. Everyone is looking out for me, I've got more than enough support. Really, I could probably use being left alone more than anything."

Penny looked hurt and Kris instantly regretted her choice of words. "I don't mean you," she said, taking her daughter's hand and pulling her fully into the quarters they'd shared until recently. "Come on, why don't I let you make me some dinner and we'll talk, okay?"

"Sounds good, mum," Penny said and started rummaging around in the small galley. Kris sank into a chair and marvelled at how what had started out as her daughter comforting her had turned itself around to the opposite.

Kris walked on to the bridge, the proposal for a new collision-avoidance protocol open on her handheld. She'd stared at it for most of the previous evening, then had finally just gone to bed when she noticed that she hadn't scrolled past the first few paragraphs. She wondered if maybe the captain was right, and she should take a few days off. But what would she do? Let Penny fuss over her and drive her insane? Hide in her quarters watching stories and brooding? She couldn't imagine anything other than work that would make her feel normal again, and so here she was taking her watch on the bridge.

Her mother hadn't been part of the bridge crew, but one of her closest friends was the navigator. Kris had grown up listening to Yolanda telling stories about the years of calculations that went into the journey, the thrill of liftoff, the terrifying first few years of the journey. Kris had found the technical talk enchanting, and a welcome relief from most of her mother's friends' discussions of old Earth, building a new society, and men. They talked a lot about men.

Kris, obviously, would never meet a man. To hear most of the members of her mother's generation talk, this was either the greatest tragedy of their circumstances or the main reason they'd volunteered for the mission. Kris didn't understand, and honestly wished they would stop talking about it. They were stuck with the reality they had, and besides, the choice they'd made to have an all-woman crew was logical.

The ship had to be a light as possible at initial launch, but they would need food for the initial journey and equipment to build a whole society. The only way to make it work was to start with just a few dozen people, but there wouldn't be enough genetic diversity among a few dozen to start a whole new chapter of humanity. Indeed, there wouldn't be among their children and grandchildren either. So it was decided.

The best answer was to launch an extensive sperm bank with an all-woman crew. Of course, it was unfair, but many more people would have liked to be aboard the *White Cloud* than it could possibly hold anyway, women and men. Necessity trumps inclusion.

Kris thought about necessity a lot. Even when she was young, she knew that she wanted to be one of the people who made the ship work. She studied science and engineering, but the concepts were like foam. The more she tried to hold on to them, the more quickly they dissolved away. She still clearly remembered a moment from her childhood: she would have been about thirteen years old and desperately struggling in school. She came home one day to find Yolanda visiting her mother. The two women were drinking spirits—a controversial act. One of the maintenance technicians had began fermenting and distilling the drink and there was a small uproar among some of the people on board. Kris was mildly shocked to see her favourite adult indulging in this new vice. Her mother, on the other hand, didn't surprise her at all.

"Hiya, kiddo," Yolanda said, slipping off the stool she'd been sitting on and coming over to Kris. She smelled a bit funny as she gave Kris a quick hug, but she let it go. "How's my future pilot?"

Kris never knew exactly what set her off. The realization that Yolanda was as human as her mother? The afternoon she'd spent sweating over a calculus problem that she still didn't understand in the least? Whatever it was, without warning her throat closed up and tears sprang to her eyes.

She was mortified. She did not want Yolanda to see her cry. She couldn't speak and still keep the tears at bay, so she just ran into the small room she had in her mother's quarters. She closed the door, flopped on to the bed, and jammed a pillow over her head. She cried as quietly as she could.

Yolanda was good about it. She and her mother left Kris alone that night and even though her mother interrogated her the next morning, Kris didn't care what she thought. She just mumbled something about hormones, her mother nodded sagely, and that was the end of it. When she ran into Yolanda in the canteen a few days later, though, Kris felt her chest tighten as soon as she saw her mother's friend standing in line for breakfast. She fought the urge to just leave, but she was hungry and if she didn't eat then she'd either be late for her physics class or she wouldn't get another chance to eat for hours. Neither option was appealing, so she swallowed her fear and got in the line.

"Maybe she won't see me," Kris thought, but as soon as Yolanda had gotten her bowl of rice and beans, their eyes met. Kris tried to pretend that she hadn't seen anything, but Yolanda came right over.

"Come sit with me," she said. "Make me forget that I'm eating *pinto gallo* for the eight hundredth day in a row."

"Uh, okay," Kris said, wishing there were some way to avoid this conversation. She got her breakfast and slipped into a chair across from Yolanda without catching her eye. She began to eat methodically.

"Have you ever met Dionne?" Yolanda asked between bites. Kris shook her head. "You know she's the ship's mate—the second in command?" Kris nodded. "She's great. Really keeps things together on the bridge. When I was studying, she used to come and give me tutorials. Not on the math and science, I was fine with all that. But about discipline, honour, service. The things that I never really had a lot of time for, but that I learned make all the difference between a successful crew and a merely competent one. Without her help I never would have become the navigator, hell I probably wouldn't have made on to the final crew list at all."

"Okay," Kris said, wondering what this reminiscence had to do with anything. She was nearly done her pinto, though, so she was pretty sure she could get away before this conversation took any more strange turns.

"Yeah, there are a lot of different skills that we need on the bridge, and once it's all up to you new generation, that's going to be even more true. I think it's easier for us in some ways. Sure, a lot of us miss home—I mean old Earth. But we all chose to be here. We're heroes, at least in our own minds." She laughed. "But your generation and those who come after have to do the real work of keeping this rust bucket running. And making sure that society stays alive, too. It's not easy, the legacy we've left you." She put down her fork and looked at Kris. She felt like Yolanda's eyes were boring into her. "I know you can do it."

She stood and picked up her breakfast dishes. As she walked away she said, "Oh yeah, and Dionne? She can't even add two and two without a computer."

"Good to see you, sir," Andie, the navigator said, slipping out of Kris's way as she headed for her desk. Andie had replaced Yolanda a few years back, shortly before Yolanda had died. Kris was still in training then, officer training at Yolanda's encouragement. She had so wanted to see Yolanda's proud face among the audience at her graduation. She was certain that if it hadn't been for that awkward breakfast, she'd have failed to gain entry to any engineering program and would have spent her life bitterly engaged in some desperate third or fourth choice job. Her mother hadn't understood what drove her, her only advice that she aim for a career doing something less challenging.

"You don't have to work so hard," she often said. "There's so much more to life than work—family, friends, love, art. Why not find something that comes easily, that you're good at, or at least that brings you joy? It's so hard to watch you struggle."

She never understood and Kris never learned how to explain it.

Kris sometimes thought that there was something fundamentally different between those who had grown up with dirt under their feet, on a planet that might have been dying but that was still inherently hospitable to life. The ship was comfortable enough, but there was never a second of doubt that, in space, life was a profoundly unnatural state.

Once in the later stages of her training, Kris spent an evening drinking with a couple of her fellow students. It must have been shortly after Yolanda died—Kris was never much of a drinker. They were talking about their parents, life, the usual things people just embarking upon adulthood tend to contemplate.

"Sometimes I think my mother has a sense of entitlement that I just can't understand," Kris said, passing the bottle across the table.

"I know," Rachel said, her head nodding as if she had no control over it. "It's like they think that there's something special about them, about all of us, really. Like the universe ought to care or something."

"They started believing all the things people said about them," Kris said, "that they were heroes, the new great explorers, saviours of humanity. I mean, come on, that's a burden and a half to carry."

They'd laughed, partly at the hubris of their parents, but also because it softened their own sorrow. Because they knew the truth. They weren't heroes, none of them. They weren't saviours, great leaders or even cowards fleeing their responsibilities to Earth. They were just people. Fallible, weak, ambitious people.

Now that Moana was dead, Kris couldn't stop herself from thinking about her mother. She must have been an ambitious woman once, she'd never had gotten aboard the *White Cloud* otherwise. Her work was certainly important; the botanical gardens which grew their food were as crucial to the success of their journey as any other part of the ship. But she never seemed to take it very seriously. She did her work, solved problems when they arose, and seemed to enjoy it enough. But it never consumed her. There was no passion, no struggle. And to Kris that felt not only too easy, but somehow mildly offensive.

To her, work had always been the most important thing she could imagine for her life. As a small child, she had played "manager" after visiting her mother at the agricultural centre. Her mother had told all her friends, laughing at how cute it was. It never felt cute to Kris—it was important preparation. This separation between her own values and her mother's apparent nonchalance covered their relationship like the kinds of fungus that Moana spent her days eradicating.

Now, as she sat at her desk on the bridge, staring blankly at a proposal she should have been able to explain in her sleep, Kris thought she maybe understood. Moana was the youngest of the initial crew members, barely in her twenties when the ship launched. It was part of the design of the mission—staggered ages as well as a diversity of skills. Someone had to be the one who would be last, and Moana had known that it would most likely be her. If it had been Kris, she would have spent her life focussed on that one fact. She would have let it define her, consume her, as she had her own position as ship's mate.

But ship's mate, while prestigious and important, was just a job. A hundred people would hold it before the journey was over. But there could be only one last hero. And, Kris realized now, it didn't mean anything. That was what her mother had been trying to tell her all along. That she and her drunken friends had been right— they were just people. They were all just people.

"Can I have a word, sir?" Kris stood at the door to the captain's study. Petra Toov looked up and smiled.

"Of course, come on in." Kris stepped though the entranceway and let the door close behind her. She settled into the seat across from the captain and fiddled with her handheld. She had never felt unsure of herself in this office. Even when she was pushing herself in training, struggling to be top of her class, she never felt that she didn't belong. The bridge, even the captain's own study, always felt more like home to her than anywhere else on the ship. Until now.

"Kris," the captain said after the silence had gone on too long. "You know I'm always here for you. Anything you need, you just let me know."

Kris bit her lower lip and nodded. She let the silence grow a little more, then said, "I never paid much attention to plants. That was mum's thing but it didn't interest me. I could never see myself anywhere but the bridge, so everything else was just a distraction."

"You're very focussed," the captain said.

"I do know a little about gardening, though," Kris went on as if the other woman hadn't said a word. "You can't live with the head of the agricultural program and not pick up on a few things. Light and shadow. That's something I know. Most plants won't thrive if they're in another, larger plant's shadow. The big one just pulls all the light, all the nutrients and the little one dies. It's normal, it's obvious, and I've known it all my life." She paused again and stared off into the middle distance. "So why did it take me so long to notice that I was trying to live in my mother's shadow? And that she spent so much of her own life trying to get out of my way?"

The captain said nothing, and Kris soon refocussed on her surroundings and gave Toov a weak smile.

"It's hard not to make history into mythology," the captain said, leaning back in her chair. "And it's hard to think you have to try to live up to a legend. I think Moana understood that, I think that was one of her great strengths." Toov laughed. "And here I go, doing it again. Making her into something larger than life. It's only going to get worse. Who knows, the ones who come later might even do it to us." She waggled her eyebrows and Kris had to laugh.

"I just wish I'd figured this all out while she was still alive," Kris said. "I never got to tell her—" Her voice caught.

"She knew," the captain said and gave Kris a moment. "Now, you take the rest of today, go home, do something for yourself. That's an order, okay?" Kris nodded. "And I will see you tomorrow."

"Thanks, captain," Kris said, standing.

"You know," the captain said, "I really prefer Petra."

"I'll try to remember that."

"Is everything all right?" Penny's look of concern was almost comical, but it made Kris feel sad.

"It really is," she said, putting a hand on her daughter's shoulder. "I just wanted to have dinner with you, spend a little time together. Is that okay with you?"

"Sure," Penny said, nodding, confusion still on her face. "You've been thinking about nan?"

Kris nodded. "I've been remembering some things she told me. About trying not to take myself so seriously. You know, lots of people used to come to ask mum's opinion on things. Not just the plants, anything. Like she had some kind of special wisdom or knowledge, just because she came from a place we'll never see."

Penny nodded. "Nan was important to a lot of people."

"She was," Kris said. "But she never saw it, never took advantage of their trust, their adoration. Most of the time when people asked her opinions, she'd end up telling them to trust their own instincts. She had a way of saying it that made them think she'd answered their question, of course, or they'd never go away. But she was always trying to get people to rely on their own intelligence. I never really noticed that's what she was doing until now."

"Nan was a great human being."

Kris smiled. "She was. But I think it's more important for me to remember not the greatness, but the humanity. That's what we need

—not heroes, not people who are larger than life, but people who are real. People like you and like me."

No-one remembers the first moment
The first deed which forced the people to think
We must leave, we must leave
No-one remembers a moment
Looking into the face of someone still standing on shore
Knowing that like a bird in a storm
We would be lost to time
Lost to space
Never to see one another again

No-one remembers because no-one wishes to remember

It was a deep darkness, a terrible choice
To take the bones of a people
As if they were merely a cargo
Not the legacy of an entire world
And fly into the darkness
With only a dream of one day
Being drawn by the light of a distant sun
To an island in the stars
A new Earth

Darusha writes science fiction and speculative poetry as M. Darusha Wehm and mainstream poetry and fiction as Darusha Wehm. Science fiction books include: *Beautiful Red*, *Children of Arkadia* and the *Andersson Dexter* cyberpunk detective series. Mainstream books include the *Devi Jones' Locker* Young Adult series and *The Home for Wayward Parrots*.

Darusha's short fiction and poetry have appeared in many venues, including *Arsenika*, *Nature*, *Escape Pod*, and several anthologies.

Originally from Canada, Darusha currently lives in Wellington, New Zealand after spending the past several years sailing the Pacific.

For more information, visit http://darusha.ca.